AR Quiz #:
B.L.: 4.4
AR Pts: 3.0

ROSA FARM

A Barnyard Tale by
Liz Wu

Illustrated by
Matt Phelan

ALFRED A. KNOPF　　NEW YORK

THIS IS A BORZOI BOOK PUBLISHED BY ALFRED A. KNOPF

Copyright © 2006 by Liz Wu
Illustrations copyright © 2006 by Matt Phelan

Published in the United States by Alfred A. Knopf, an imprint of Random House Children's Books, a division of Random House, Inc., New York.

KNOPF, BORZOI BOOKS, and the colophon are registered trademarks of Random House, Inc.

www.randomhouse.com/kids

Educators and librarians, for a variety of teaching tools, visit us at www.randomhouse.com/teachers

Library of Congress Cataloging-in-Publication Data
Wu, Liz.
Rosa farm : a barnyard tale / by Liz Wu ; illustrated by Matt Phelan. — 1st ed.
p. cm.
SUMMARY: With his father away at the fair, a young rooster must crow to bring the sun up, but when the geese play a mean trick on him and then kidnap his little sister, it takes several of the farm animals working together to teach the geese a lesson.
ISBN-13: 978-0-375-83681-7 (trade) — ISBN-13: 978-0-375-93681-4 (lib. bdg.)
ISBN-10: 0-375-83681-0 (trade) — ISBN-10: 0-375-93681-5 (lib. bdg.)
[1. Roosters—Fiction. 2. Chickens—Fiction. 3. Geese—Fiction. 4. Domestic animals—Fiction. 5. Farm life—Fiction.] I. Phelan, Matt, ill. II. Title.
PZ7.W9622Ro 2006 [Fic]—dc22 2006001279

Printed in the United States of America

10 9 8 7 6 5 4 3 2 1

First Edition

For Linda

Contents

Chapter 1

The News

*I*n a tucked-away corner of the world, in a land full of sun, on an almost forgotten plot of earth, sat Rosa Farm. On a Saturday afternoon, as during every summer afternoon, the farm was usually quiet because it was too hot to do anything. Even Lester the dog, who was usually busy making sure everything was in order, would be curled up next to the fishpond or panting on the stoop with his long tongue almost touching the ground.

On this particular Saturday afternoon, however, there was something stirring in the air. It was like a bottle fly buzzing from one stall to another, landing with a tickle and then moving away quickly before being spotted. There was a rumor going around, and even on the hottest and laziest of summer days, word can travel fast.

Eli, a sleek black cat as quiet as a shadow, was always the first to find out about any news. Today, instead of going for his usual nap under the lime trees, Eli went straight to the fishpond, where the geese usually spent the afternoons cooling off. He could hear them already, gossiping about farm life, gabbing about everyone's business, or possible business. It was nothing new—just shameless talk about the prissy pony or the half-deaf sheep.

"Who does she think she is?" demanded Babble, a goose with an extremely long neck. "A princess? Priscilla prances around like she's on a stage, trying to attract an audience."

"Yeah!" agreed Gabble, a goose with a short black stripe on her bright orange beak. "She's such a snob. But what about that sheep? Ever try to talk with her?"

"Eh?" squawked Babble. "Could you repeat that?" They burst into a strange honking sort of laughter that resembled rush-hour traffic in the big city.

"And her new neighbor isn't much better," chimed in Prattle, a goose with shiny, dark, beady eyes and a terrible mean streak. "Cesar the scaredy-pig! Woo-hoo! He should have been born a mouse or a rabbit. He should have—"

"Excuse me," interrupted Eli, annoyed by their never-ending gossip. "I have something that may interest you."

Prattle turned and hissed. "What could you have that would possibly concern us, cat?"

Eli stared at him coolly. "Information," he said. "For the price of a fish."

"Is it news?" asked Babble eagerly.

"Is it fresh?" Eli snapped.

Gabble, who was tired of repeating the same worn-out stories and couldn't wait to sink her beak into a juicy piece of information, honked impatiently. She dove into the pool, coming out a moment later with a splash and a slender, shiny fish wriggling in her big orange beak.

"Let's hear it," said Prattle. The geese crowded around. "And if you want that fish," he added, "this had better be good."

Within a matter of minutes, the farmyard exploded. Babble, Gabble, and Prattle burst upon the sleeping animals like a sudden storm. They ran from pen to pen, spreading the news with the speed of wildfire.

Chapter 2

The Chickens

 "Wake up!" cried Pepina, nudging her older brother. Pepina was a fluffy and slightly impatient chick. "I'm not sleeping," he grunted. "What is it?"

Gallileon, who had been counting ants in a haystack, had just slipped into a light doze when Pepina woke him. He hated being interrupted, and he certainly wasn't going to admit to having been caught napping.

"Well, if you're awake," said Pepina, "then why haven't you paid any attention to the news?"

"What news? What are you talking about?" asked Gallileon sleepily.

Pepina rolled her eyes and sighed loudly. "If you haven't been sleeping, you must have been in another world. The geese have been shouting about it all afternoon!"

"About what?" Gallileon teased. "Your pretty little bow?"

Pepina glared at him. A few days ago, while digging for bugs, she had found a cute red-and-white polka-dot bow. Pepina wore her new prize possession around her neck to help cover up her unruly feathers. "Find out for yourself, then," she said angrily, turning to leave.

"Okay, I'm sorry," Gallileon said with a giggle. "It's just that, well, you know how those geese are. You can't believe anything they say."

"Fine, Mr. Smarty-Pants," Pepina said. "But it would be a big shame if you were the very last one on the farm to find out that Farmer Rosa is taking Papa to the fair tomorrow."

"To where?" Gallileon asked excitedly.

Pepina hopped away. Before she disappeared behind the fence, she looked back smugly and said, "Papa has been chosen to compete with all the other roosters in the area to see who's the best one. If you weren't so busy studying the ants in the haystack, maybe you could go and wish him luck. Oh yeah, and Mama wants to talk with you."

"Hey, wait, Pepina!" shouted Gallileon. "Don't go. I . . ."

But she already had.

Gallileon stood, stunned for a moment, taking in the news. Then he ran as fast as his spindly rooster legs could carry him. He ducked under the fence, making sure not to disturb Bartholomew, the grumpy old billy goat, who was munching on some dried weeds. In the distance, he could hear the geese shouting out the news. He scurried through a hole in the chicken wire, fluttered over a pile of wood, tore across the dusty yard, and almost knocked over his mother, who was serving his sisters their supper.

Leila smiled at him. "I see you've heard the news," she said. "Eat your dinner, and then we'll talk about it."

Gallileon, who was out of breath, eyed the three worms wiggling in the dust. Without further ado, he scooped them up and swallowed them in one gulp. Then he ran over to the water bowl and washed them down. He raced back, in a hurry to hear what was going on.

Before he could say a word, Leila gave him a firm look and said, "Not now; it would be too much for

your sisters." Pepina gave him a knowing smirk. Leila nodded to her right and said, "Go and wait for me at the back of the coop."

Gallileon glanced at the downy pile of fuzzy, golden heads bobbing up and down as they tugged on their worms. One chick pulled so hard that the one holding the other end let go, sending the first one tumbling backward with a loud, startled "Cheep!!!"

Gallileon smiled as he helped her up, made a face at Pepina, then went to the back of the coop, chuckling softly and trembling with excitement.

Chapter 3

The Request

Wispy clouds trailed like cobwebs in the slowly darkening sky. Gallileon settled into a corner of the fence and gazed up at the horizon. He could hear the usual suppertime sounds—the mooing of Felicity the cow, the tiny peeps of his sisters, and the shameful whining of Lester begging for table scraps.

Gallileon breathed deeply, letting out a happy squawk. It was a good life here. The Rosas were kind caretakers. The animals didn't have to worry about being sold or eaten, because Farmer Rosa considered them all members of his household. He would no sooner sell them than his grandchildren.

Each animal on the farm was aware of its good fortune and contributed something toward its keep. The cow gave milk, the chickens gave eggs, the ducks and geese gave feathers, the pony gave rides, the dog gave orders, the sheep gave wool, the donkey carried heavy loads, and the fish kept the pond clean. The goat, pig, and cat were exempt—the goat because of old age and the other two because they were guests. Cesar and Eli belonged to Mrs. Rosa's sister, who was ill and couldn't look after them. Since they were guests, they couldn't be expected to do anything, although Gallileon figured the cat probably caught mice.

As for roosters, Gallileon thought, puffing up his chest, they were important because . . . because . . . *Wait a minute,* he thought. *What am I good for?*

Gallileon was stumped. Whenever he was puzzled, he scratched at the ground. He was so involved with his digging and scratching he didn't notice Leila, even when she was standing right behind him.

"Didn't you get enough to eat?" she asked. She thought he was looking for more worms.

Gallileon jumped high into the air. "What?" he cried. "No! I mean, yes! I mean, I'm not hungry," he said, embarrassed. "I was just thinking."

"Sorry to interrupt you," said Leila, grinning. "I bet you're terribly excited about Papa going to the fair tomorrow."

The fair! He had almost forgotten about the fair! What would Papa be doing there? And then there was the other question: What were roosters good for? Tongue-tied, Gallileon just nodded his head.

Leila laughed. "I have a favor to ask of you. It's for your father."

"Where *is* Papa?" asked Gallileon. He had not seen his father all day.

"I'm afraid Magellan won't be back until tomorrow night," Leila said. "The farmers are keeping him indoors so that he doesn't get dusty."

Gallileon's heart dropped with disappointment. "But," he argued weakly, "I just found out. I didn't get a chance—"

"Don't you worry about that," she said. "You can be a big help to him in another way."

"Really? How? And when?" asked Gallileon, hopping up into the air. He was always eager to help his father. In fact, more than anything in the world, he wanted to grow up to be like Magellan, to stand tall and shake out his beautiful mahogany feathers, and slowly pace around the farmyard with dignity and grace. He was so caught up in imagining his spindly legs growing stronger, his brick-red feathers darkening, his chest filling out, and his wobble of a walk becoming a steady stride that he didn't hear his mother speaking to him until she asked, "So, will you do it?"

"Of course," Gallileon replied. "Uh . . . do what?"

Leila sighed. "Didn't you hear *anything* I just said?" At Gallileon's blank look, she used her best scolding tone and said, "You really should pay attention because this is a very important job."

Gallileon's eyes lit up. Something important!

"Do you know how Papa gets up early every morning and stands on the fence?" she asked.

"Oh yes!" replied Gallileon, who had often wondered why his father always got up so early.

"Do you know what he does there?" Leila asked.

"Well, he goes up there and crows," said Gallileon, feeling there was probably a better answer.

Leila gave him a funny look. "Yes, but do you know why?"

Gallileon scratched at the ground. He didn't like to admit he hadn't a clue. He had never thought to ask why his father crowed at dawn any more than he had thought to ask why they ate worms for supper. It just seemed a natural thing to do in the morning, like yawning and stretching. Maybe, thought Gallileon, it was a form of exercise. "Is it a way to keep his voice in shape?" Gallileon wondered.

Leila laughed so hard she had to shut her eyes. She smoothed out her feathers, still chuckling, and said, "Heavens no! Papa goes out there every morning to bring in the new day. He wakes while it is still dark and joins the songbirds in singing the day into being."

Could all roosters do this thing his father did? Or was it something passed down from rooster to rooster for generations? Was *this* what roosters were good for? Gallileon felt like crowing with joy. It was like discovering a magical power.

Leila cleared her throat. "Your father calls the sun each morning and invites him to shine. He welcomes each new day and lets everyone else on the farm know that tomorrow has arrived," she explained.

"That sounds like a very important job!" Gallileon said. He was beginning to feel like he might explode with enthusiasm.

"It is," Leila agreed. "Think about it. The sun, which makes the plants grow, which gives us light to see by, which keeps us warm, whose coming and going marks each day—"

"Does Papa bring the sun?" Gallileon asked.

"*Herald* would be a better word," said Leila.

"What's that mean?" asked Gallileon.

Pepina's shrill voice cut through the conversation. "Ma, come quick!" she yelled. "Elena saw a weird shadow. She thinks it's a fox. I think she's nuts, but all the little ones are crying."

Leila stood up to go. "So, can you do that tomorrow, Gallileon? Wake up before dawn and sing to the sun? The whole farm would appreciate it."

Gallileon was a jumble of emotions: excitement, wonder, and confusion. "Sure!" he said, puffing up his chest with pride. "I just have a few questions."

Leila was already on her way inside the coop. "Thank you, Gallileon. We knew we could count on you," she said. "Papa will be very pleased." And then she was gone.

Gallileon, head spinning, flew to the westernmost fence post and took in the splendid sight of the glowing sun spreading its last few rays over the farmyard. As he stood gazing into the horizon, he felt as if he were dissolving into the golden ball of light, sinking into a soft bed of colorful clouds. He watched as the sky grew richer and dimmer, as the shadows on the ground grew longer and stranger, as the air all around became chiller and stiller, until he all but melted into the silence that surrounded him.

Chapter 4

The Test

When Lester made his nightly rounds to check that everything was in order and all were in bed, he trotted right past Gallileon, who, standing very still, simply made the fence post's shadow a tiny bit longer. Gallileon was deep in thought.

First of all, he thought about his father. Everyone liked Magellan. He had a quiet, friendly personality that made everyone respect him. He was handsome, too, with bright eyes, a powerful chest, sturdy legs, perfectly clean feathers, and a beautiful tail the color of autumn leaves.

Gallileon, who was at the awkward age of being not quite a full-grown rooster, was tired of his spindly legs and his wild feathers, which seemed to grow every which way and stick out in the most unflattering places. What's more, they were red! Not a deep, rich, dark auburn, but flaming red, like the inside of a brick! He was too skinny, his beak too thin and pointy, and his eyes too big for his narrow head. Gallileon felt like a walking feather duster. Whenever he complained about his looks to his mother, she just brushed him aside, saying that he would fill out when he grew up. He could hardly wait.

Gallileon wondered how Magellan was able to call forth the sun each day. It didn't seem possible that the sun, so big and far away in the sky, could ever hear a tiny rooster on a farm. And yet, Gallileon thought, if anyone was fit for the job, it was Magellan. He strutted back and forth on the fence with a glow of satisfaction. "Now," he crowed softly to himself, preening his chest feathers, "it's my turn!" He decided it would be a good idea to practice first. So . . . where to start?

Step one: Jump onto the fence. *That's handy,* thought Gallileon. *I'm already there!* Now for step two: Hmmmm . . . what was it Magellan did? He stood up straight and cocked his head to the sky. Right. Gallileon puffed out his shaggy chest and stretched his beak up until his neck began to ache. *A little uncomfortable, but simple enough,* he thought. Now for step three: A deep breath. Gallileon sucked in as much air as he could hold, raising his wings as he filled his lungs. He stood on his toes and got ready for the crow, but on the brink of his cry, he paused at a strange noise.

Gallileon's heart jumped into his throat at the sound of footsteps. *Oh no!* he thought, realizing Lester was back, making his second set of rounds. *He must have heard something!* Lester was moving slowly, suspiciously, sniffing the air as he neared the fence.

Gallileon, trembling with the effort of holding his breath, wished with all his might for the dog to go away. Lester stopped for a moment and scratched slowly, as if deciding what to do. Then he began to scratch harder. Then he began rubbing as hard as a bear against the fence. Gallileon looked down in horror, trying to keep his balance on the pole. Suddenly, just as Gallileon felt he might faint, Lester's ears pricked up, and he growled softly. He bounded across the farmyard, disappearing as quickly and as quietly as he had come.

Gallileon fluttered down to the ground in relief. *Phew! That was a close call,* he thought. *If I had crowed then, not only would Lester have heard me, but I might have woken up the whole farm. What a situation that would have been!* Gallileon decided to go to bed before he got into any trouble. He would just have to practice in the morning.

Then a most worrisome thought hit him: What if he overslept?

If he failed tomorrow, it might upset the whole routine of the farm. Maybe the farmer would miss the fair. Maybe the cow wouldn't produce milk. Maybe Leila would be too upset to lay eggs. Maybe the donkey would feel too lazy to carry loads and the pony too grumpy to give rides. Even worse: What if the sun didn't rise? What if it skipped Rosa Farm, or even just stayed in its bed of comfy clouds, leaving the entire world in darkness?

This was turning out to be more complicated than he expected.

That does it! Gallileon thought. *I'll just have to stay out here until morning. When it's over, I can always snooze in the haystack, but not a moment before. There's too much at stake.*

So he waited. Gallileon sat very still and breathed in the night air, which smelled like fresh-cut roses drizzled with dew. It seemed as if the farm, though quiet as usual, were bubbling with a slow, invisible, growing pressure, like the feeling right before a thunderstorm.

Trembling, Gallileon brushed some leaves and

dried grass into a pile and settled down upon it. *I must try and relax,* he thought. He wiggled into the leaves and began to see in his mind the new life he would begin tomorrow—as a grown-up rooster! He sighed deeply, imagining his legs growing longer, his feathers growing darker, his voice deepening, and his chest filling out.

Chapter 5

The Moment of Truth

Gallileon had the nagging feeling that something was wrong. It seemed like only a moment had passed since he'd sat down to wait. Now something was stirring at the edge of his mind, and he couldn't make out what it was. Drowsily, he opened an eye. It was still dark. Then, in a flash, he recognized those little sounds that had tickled his dreams and forced him to wake: birds singing!

Gallileon sprang to his feet, but his legs promptly gave way beneath him. He was achy and numb. *Oh no!* he thought with a pang of panic. *I fell asleep!* Slowly, painfully, he stood up and looked around. It was too dark to see anything. *Of course it's dark!* he thought angrily. *I haven't brought the sun out yet! Oh dear, how long have those birds been singing?*

Gallileon made his way clumsily up to the post

he had chosen the night before. Hurriedly, in three jerky motions, he craned his head, inhaled sharply, and let loose an enormous "CROAK!"

Priscilla the pony, who was nearest to that side of the fence, stirred in her pen uneasily. "What on earth was that?" she mumbled.

Gallileon choked with surprise and embarrassment. *Gosh, I hope nobody heard that!* he thought. He strained his eyes, looking for any change in the darkness before him. He shook his head. *It's no wonder,* he thought. *That certainly won't do!*

He took a mighty breath and tried again. And again. He tried holding the sound out a little longer. He tried making his voice go deeper. When that didn't work, he tried three short cries in a row. Five in a row. Seven in a row.

By this time, all the animals on the farm, except the sheep, whose deafness worked in her favor, were turning in their sleep and casting a weary eye toward the still-black sky. Pepina, one of the few who knew what was going on, buried her head deeply under the straw and vowed to get back at Gallileon for messing up her sleep. Bartholomew the goat, who liked to sleep late, was very upset. "Confound that crazy rooster!" he bleated. "What in tarnation is he up to?"

Gallileon fell to the ground, completely exhausted. He was out of breath, and his throat hurt. "Now what do I do?" he groaned. "I fell asleep and messed everything up. If the sun doesn't come, and it's all my fault, then what?" He sighed and turned sadly toward the chicken coop, defeated.

As he took his first step, Gallileon almost fell over with shock. The sky! It was lighter! He closed one eye, and then the other, checking with each to make sure it was not just wishful seeing. Without a doubt, the sky, which had been pitch-black when he had jumped down, was now a pale sort of gray.

Without a second thought, Gallileon shot up the fence post and crowed with all his heart, "Cock-a-doodle-dooooooooo!" Slowly the sky began to change. The gray grew lighter, and soon he was able to see the outline of thin clouds and eventually even a little pink. Gallileon crowed until he was blue in the face. He had done it! Morning had come!

He had just begun to enjoy his victory when another bombshell hit him: Where was the sun?!

Quickly, Gallileon looked to the left and to the right, carefully searching every bit of sky in sight for even a glimmer of gold. With so few clouds, there was nowhere for the sun to hide.

Gallileon threw his wings up in despair. Now what was the matter? Had he crowed too loudly and been rude to the sun? Was it angry with him or confused by his voice, which was different from Magellan's? Was this test ever going to end?

Painfully, Gallileon got down from the fence post one last time. Each step felt like he was walking through mud as he trudged to bed. Even though he was numb and stiff from spending the night outside, he felt the gentle touch of something warm on his feathertips. While he had been crowing with all his might toward the west, the sun had been sneaking up behind him in the east! If he had been any less tired, he could have kicked himself. As it was, though, he could barely stumble back to the chicken coop and fall in a heap on his soft straw bed.

"Good job," snickered Pepina.

Chapter 6

A Family Breakfast

Gallileon stepped groggily out into the late-morning light to find Leila and the chicks pecking around in the chicken yard. From the sound of things, she was teaching them how to hunt for worms. Mmmmmm, that reminded him: He was dying of hunger! With lightning speed, he caught a beetle, a few ants, a tasty white grub of some sort, and a rather tough, stringy worm. He gobbled them all down as fast as he found them. When he finished, he looked up to see his mother and sisters gathered around him, watching.

"Well, look who's finally up," said Pepina. "Good morning—or should I say good day?"

"Hello, darling," said Leila. "I've been showing the girls how to look for food, and you do it so well."

"It's a good thing, too, with his appetite," Pepina giggled.

Gallileon ignored her. He swallowed down a shiny green beetle.

Leila turned toward her small, fluffy daughters. "Survival is the most important thing one can learn," she continued. "And being able to find your own worms is the first sign of being grown-up."

"Hey!" cried Pepina. "I found a June bug. Doesn't that count for something?"

"Of course it does," Leila said, "but you'll need to find a lot more than that if you're going to provide for your own chicks someday."

"Oh yeah, I forgot. Gallileon only has to take care of himself," Pepina said smugly.

"Gallileon has other tasks," Leila replied. "Speaking of which, I want you all to know what a great job he did calling the sun this morning while Papa was away. Let's all congratulate him."

The younger sisters chirped happily while Pepina frowned and muttered, "You call *that* singing?"

"Pepina!" Leila gave her a warning look.

"Okay, okay!" Pepina cried. She looked at Gallileon, fluttered her eyelashes, and said in a squeaky voice, "Thank you, dear brother, for your beaaaaaaautiful singing this morning."

"My pleaaaaaaasure, dear sister. I never knew you cared." Gallileon chuckled. He thought Pepina was terribly funny when she was angry.

She continued, raising her voice even higher, "Every croak was music to my ears. I had to bury my head under the straw because I couldn't bear to hear such lovely—"

Leila poked Pepina with her wing. "That's enough," she said dryly. "You're supposed to be an example to your younger sisters, but all you're teaching them is how to be bad-tempered. Perhaps it would be best if you spent some time with your older brother and learned how to get along."

"Oh, Mama!" cried Gallileon and Pepina in unison. They looked at each other in horror.

"Don't talk back to me," she snapped. "You've had your breakfast; now go and play. I don't want to see you away from his side before the afternoon is up, Pepina. And by the way, Gallileon," she added sweetly, "I'll send Papa to speak to you tonight, and you can tell him how it went. You're growing up to be quite a fine young rooster. I'm sure he will be proud."

Blushing, all Gallileon could do was stammer

"Thank you" and turn toward the fence. With Leila's words and the tiny peeps of his sisters ringing in his ears, he started walking, with Pepina trailing slowly and sulkily behind him.

Chapter 7

Pepina's Big Leap

Pepina nudged her big brother. "Now what do we do, oh wise one?" she asked.

"Why don't you tell me?" he said. "You're the one who got us into this."

"Well, sooooorrrry, Mr. Sensitive!" said Pepina. "I was just trying to be nice. See if I ever compliment your voice again."

Gallileon rolled his eyes. "I don't know what we're going to do," he said, thinking out loud, "but one thing's for sure—we have to get out of here." He hopped over to a stack of crates piled by the corner of the fence.

"Why don't you just go through the hole in the fence like everyone else?" Pepina asked.

"Because," said Gallileon, "the hole is way over there, and we can get out easily right here."

"Maybe *you* can," she said sharply, "but not me. It's too high up. And even if I could get up there somehow, I couldn't get down because I'm too small."

"All the more reason to grow up, then," Gallileon teased. "So why don't you go through the hole?"

Pepina stamped with frustration. "Because you wouldn't wait for me. I know it," she said.

"So?" asked Gallileon, enjoying his sister's annoyance. "Why would you care?"

As much as Gallileon got on her nerves, Pepina was secretly very curious to find out what he did during the day, and she was also getting bored of trying to play with her sisters, who could barely even talk yet. But there was no way she was going to admit this to her older brother. "We'd get in trouble," she replied lamely.

"We're already in trouble, remember?" Gallileon laughed. "I think the real reason you're upset is because you'd miss me!" he joked.

Pepina glared at him, her fluffy cheeks puffed out in anger. "Hardly," she replied coldly. "I couldn't care less if I never saw you again."

"All right, all right," Gallileon said, trying to control his giggling. "Tell you what. I'm going up and over the fence, so if you want to come, you can climb onto my back while I jump. And if you're too scared, you can stay here and tell Mama I left you. Then I'd be the one in trouble. How does that sound?"

"I'm not scared!" Pepina shouted, hopping onto his back.

Up they went. The first crate was low to the ground and easy to reach. The second crate was a bit higher and took a little flapping to climb. As Gallileon beat his wings, Pepina hung on tight with her little claws, watching the ground below swing back and forth as if she were dangling on a string. The third crate was higher still. Gallileon puffed and crowed as he struggled up. By the time they got to the top, Pepina was green with motion sickness.

"Now for the easy part!" Gallileon yelled, leaping over the fence. Pepina closed her eyes and held on for dear life. In a moment, they landed with a THUMP, and Pepina rolled off, gasping for breath. She lay on the ground and looked up at the sky. That had been the most terrifying experience she had ever had. But it was also the most exciting. Part of her wanted to do it again. Perhaps spending the day with Gallileon wouldn't be as bad as she had thought. Maybe it would even be fun.

Gallileon grinned as she stood slowly and

brushed herself off. "So, it was a little rough, huh?" he said.

Pepina drew herself up to her full four-inch height and declared, "It was a piece of cake."

"Good," replied Gallileon, "because there's more cake to come." Then he began walking. Pepina followed after him, unusually silent.

Chapter 8

A Less-than-Friendly Encounter

Gallileon walked aimlessly around the farmyard with Pepina hopping quietly behind him. Across the way, Bartholomew the goat stuck his head out of his pen and blew raspberries at them. He seemed to be extremely upset about something.

Gallileon took no notice. The old goat was usually grumpy. Pepina, who had never seen the goat so close before, was startled by his bleating and stamping. She edged closer to Gallileon, then turned and made rude faces back to prove she wasn't afraid.

Next they walked past Burro the donkey's pen. Burro blinked at them lazily. He did not normally concern himself with chickens, or any other animal for that matter.

"This is boring!" Pepina said. "We're just walking in a big circle. If we were visiting someone, that would be one thing, but we're just wandering around. And none of these animals has any manners!"

"Shush," said Gallileon. "We're saying hi to Cesar." Gallileon knew the pig was new to the farm and figured he might like to make friends.

Cesar, a small white pig with a brown spot on one side, was sitting very still in a puddle of water near his trough.

"He isn't moving," whispered Pepina. "Is he even awake?"

"Of course I'm awake," snorted Cesar, who had unusually good hearing. "Whoever heard of sleeping in a puddle?"

"I beg your pardon," said Gallileon, "for my sister's bad manners. We're just out for a walk, so we thought we'd say hi. My name is Gallileon, and this is my sister Pepina."

"A pleasure," greeted the pig with a little bow of his head. "My name is Cesar. So delighted to meet you. I hardly ever get visitors! Excuse me for not being prepared for company. I'm just having a swim."

"But you're not moving!" Pepina protested.

"All right," admitted Cesar, "I'm having a dip, then. If I move, the water turns to mud. And whoever heard of taking a bath in mud?"

Cesar was quite an unusual pig in that he was extremely clean. His pen was the tidiest on the farm, and his skin was always spotless. Except, of course, for the spot he had been born with, which wouldn't wash off no matter how hard he tried.

"Oh, I see," said Pepina. "Your skin shines beautifully," she added.

"Why, thank you," said Cesar, grinning modestly. "You look very nice yourself with that pretty bow."

Cesar and Pepina liked each other right away. Gallileon shifted from one foot to the other. *What girly talk!* he thought, bored. Then he had an idea. Maybe he could leave Pepina with her new friend and sneak off on his own.

But the moment Gallileon was going to make his getaway, Cesar said, "I hear someone coming! Sounds like three or four of them."

Gallileon and Pepina looked down the yard. If they strained their eyes, they could make out tiny shapes bobbing slowly into sight. Cesar snorted and said, "They're ducks!"

"Ducks!" cried Pepina and Gallileon in unison. Their feathers stood on end in alarm. On Rosa Farm, the chickens and ducks were bitter rivals. It had started long before Gallileon's time, when the ducks, jealous of the special attention the chickens received from the farmers, began to play cruel tricks on them. They put sand in the chicken feed and foul-smelling fish in the drinking water. They could be bullies, too. Magellan had told his children to stay away from ducks, and now here was a bunch heading straight for them!

"Three ducks," Cesar whispered, "and one goose!"

"A goose, huh?" Gallileon mumbled. He didn't know if that was good or bad. Geese were bigger than ducks, but they didn't really have anything against chickens. Also, geese were the news reporters of the farm, so if the ducks tried anything, there would be witnesses. Those ducks wouldn't dare pick a fight, Gallileon decided. Still, he was nervous.

The four shapes were clearly visible now, marching quickly in a diamond formation. The goose was in the lead with a duck on either side and another duck in back.

Gallileon swallowed hard. How should he act? Bold? Bored? He turned to Cesar and struck up some small talk. "So, uh," he said, trying to hide his nervousness, "nice weather we're having."

Cesar, who was quite bright, understood immediately. "Oh yes, I agree," he said.

They chatted about this and that—the pleasant smell of the roses, how yummy the corn was this year, and other such niceties. The yard was dead quiet. Gallileon hoped with all his might that the ducks had passed them by. He was just about to look when he heard a gruff, nasal voice say, "Well, dearies, what have we here? A rooster, a chick, and a pig. Is there a party going on that we haven't heard about?"

Gallileon turned. His heart sank when he saw that the goose in command was Prattle, the meanest of the three geese.

"Oh, it's you," Gallileon said coolly. "Hi."

"Aren't you going to invite us to join you?" asked the first duck, whose name was Dip. He was brown and green and a little pudgy.

"Yeah, don't you have any manners?" added Flip, the second duck. He was also brown and green but was as skinny as a rail.

"I doubt it, boys. It seems we're not welcome here," said the last duck with a hiss. His name was Nip. He was white, like a goose, and mean, like Prattle.

"Do what you want." Gallileon shrugged. "This is a public place."

"Of course it is," said Dip. "You don't own the farm."

"Yeah," said Flip. "You roosters go around like you think you're kings, but you're not."

"You're just noisemakers!" hooted Nip.

Cesar spoke hotly, "And you're just troublemakers! Why don't you go and pick on one of your own kind?"

"Who asked for your opinion, pig?" snapped Dip.

"If we want to hear from you, we'll let you know. Got it?" snarled Flip.

"Let it slide," snickered Nip. "He's only butting in 'cause he don't know any better. If he were smart, he would know to keep his trap shut. But, unfortunately, all pigs are naturally stupid. Aren't you?" he said, turning to Cesar. "Go on and say something to prove how dumb you are."

Cesar glared at him in silence.

Gallileon looked around for a way to escape. It did not look good. He and Pepina were surrounded, with Dip and Flip on either side of them and Nip and Prattle straight ahead.

Chapter 9

The Challenge

"**L**ads, lads, calm down," said Prattle in a voice as smooth as a snake getting ready to strike. "It's no wonder we haven't been invited to their party—we don't belong. See?"

The ducks laughed noisily as if Prattle had just shared a private joke. Prattle went on, "The pig, the rooster, and the chick all have something in common that we don't."

"What's that, boss?" asked Dip, enjoying the game.

"The thing that these three animals share," said Prattle, grinning, "is that they are completely useless! The chick, at least, has an excuse. One day she'll grow up to be a little egg-making factory, just like her mama. But the other two are worth about as much as a couple of well-fed rats!"

The goose and the ducks then burst into a chorus

of laughter so loud and vicious that even the sheep looked out of her pen in curiosity. Gallileon was shocked. Cesar gasped as though he had been struck. And Pepina, who had been trying her best to keep silent the whole time, could hold it in no longer. She turned to the nearest duck, which happened to be Flip, and clamped her beak on his leg.

"Ow!" he yelled, looking around to see what had bit him. The others stopped laughing and looked at him in surprise.

Pepina, who was only getting started, climbed up on Gallileon's back so that she would be closer to the height of the others. "First of all," she yelled, "my mother is *not* an egg factory! How dare you talk about her like that!" She glared at the ducks and pointed at them with her tiny wings. "Secondly," she continued, "Cesar is smarter than all of you goons put together. What would you know about pigs, anyway? You spend all your days with your heads underwater, so you probably have mud for brains!"

The ducks stared at her, amazed that such a little pile of fluff could have such a temper.

Pepina still wasn't finished. "And as for being useful," she shouted, "all you do is shed your stinky feathers! How many feathers does it take to stuff a pillow? A lot, and they have to be washed first to get

the slime off." She took a deep breath, gathering steam. She had a feeling she shouldn't say the next thing she had lined up, but it was only fair to stick up for her brother, too. Besides, she was on a roll.

"Finally," she cried, looking each bird squarely in the eye, "the only reason you're picking on Gallileon is because you're jealous. Not only is he better-looking than you, but he happens to have the most important job on the entire farm—waking up the sun! If it weren't for him, it would still be nighttime, and you would have to swim in the dark in your smelly pond!" Then she smiled. "But it's not your fault," she said, "because you didn't know better. After all, geese and ducks are naturally idiots." She patted Dip on the head for good measure. "There, there," she laughed.

Flip, furious, tried to bite her, but Pepina was too small and quick. She slid down Gallileon's back and stood beneath him with her wings folded.

"Just wait till you're on your own, missy," growled Dip.

"If I were you, I wouldn't set foot outside the fence again," sneered Flip.

"'Cause whenever you do, we'll be waiting . . . to teach you some manners," snarled Nip.

Prattle had to admit he admired Pepina's bravery. None of his fellow geese or any of the ducks ever dared to stand up to him or show that they had a mind of their own. He felt a rare tinge of respect for the chick. He even thought he might like to have her for a friend. He was bored of the nonstop chatter of the geese and of directing the slow-witted ducks. Secretly, he was quite lonely. He longed for a companion who was smart and fearless, like Pepina. Even so, he couldn't let a little chick make a fool of him.

So he thought about it, and as he thought, he remembered something the cat had told him earlier in the morning in exchange for an even bigger fish than before. Suddenly, his face lit up with a cunning smile. *Ah!* he thought. *I have the perfect plan.*

"Come, friends, let's not bicker," Prattle said sweetly. "We meant no harm, did we, boys?"

The ducks looked at him, confused.

"We apologize if we seemed a bit rude," continued Prattle, his voice dripping with poisonous honey. "We never meant to ruffle anyone's feathers. Let's just forget about all this and go our merry ways, shall we?"

Gallileon sighed with relief.

"Still," Prattle said, with the look of a cat that has cornered its prey, "it is news to us, and everyone knows how we love news, to hear that Gallileon is now a grown-up rooster. We thought only Magellan brought in the sun every morning. It appears we were wrong. Please forgive us."

The ducks cackled, thinking that this was another joke. Prattle turned to them and hissed. They stopped in mid-laugh, their beaks hanging open. Gallileon would have found it funny if he didn't have the feeling that something was about to go terribly wrong.

"So would you mind," asked Prattle, "giving a little demonstration?"

"A what?" said Gallileon.

"Well, if you really called the sun this morning, then we would like to see how you did it." Prattle smiled.

What was the goose up to? "How can I do that," Gallileon asked, "when the sun is already up in the sky?"

"Good point," Prattle admitted. "Well, of course, you wouldn't have to repeat it exactly, since the sun *is* already out. But we can't wait until tomorrow because Magellan's coming back and will be taking over again. Are we right?"

"So what exactly is it that you want?" asked Gallileon uneasily.

"Just a little demonstration," said Prattle, grinning like a crocodile. "We know you did it, because the proof is in the sky. We are just curious about *how* you did it. All we're asking is for you to give a few stout crows, exactly as you did before, that's all. It would liven things up around here, as well as let everyone know how grown-up you've become so that you are paid the respect you deserve."

"I don't know," said Gallileon. "I don't really see the point."

Prattle cleared his throat, pretending to be hurt. "The *point,* my dear, is simply to take credit for the wonderful job you've done. It would be a great honor for us geese to be the first to spread the word about you. Imagine! 'Magellan the Magnificent and his gallant son, Gallileon, the ruby-feathered prince of Rosa Farm!' It has a ring to it, don't you think?"

"I think he's scared," said Dip. "He's got stage fright."

"I think he's a liar," said Flip. "He probably never did nothing. It was Magellan all along, before he went to the fair this morning."

"I think he's really a hen dressed up as a rooster," said Nip. "So why don't you go and lay some eggs? Heh heh!"

"My, my!" Prattle laughed. "Well, which is it, my good sir—are you the son of the great Magellan, or are you a lying baby wannabe with sticks for legs and big bug eyes?"

"That's a dirty trick!" yelled Pepina.

"Quiet, squirt!" snarled Nip. "This has nothing to do with you."

Gallileon scratched at the ground. It looked like there was no way out of this. Either he gave the goose what he wanted, or he had to live being known as a fake, which was even worse than being a failure.

"I dare you," challenged Dip.

"I double-dare you," shouted Flip.

"I triple-*dog*-dare you," hollered Nip.

"That is not necessary," laughed Prattle. "I can tell by the fire in his eyes that he will not disappoint." He turned and nodded toward the well, which stood in the center of the farm, between the two rows of pens. If the farm were a town, the well would be its main square. "We'll meet there at high noon," he said, "so come ready for action." Then, suddenly, Prattle turned and started back toward the pond, with the three cackling ducks marching behind him.

Chapter 10

A Moment to Prepare

Gallileon watched the white and brown shapes shrink away in the distance. The sun had already risen almost above his head. He didn't have much time to get ready.

Cesar grunted. "Bullies, all of them!" he said angrily. "Someone ought to teach them a lesson!" When he saw Gallileon's pale face, he tried to be comforting. "Don't worry, Gallileon," he said gently. "You will do fine. Just repeat what you did this morning."

Gallileon choked. "What I did this morning? Didn't you hear me?" he cried. "You have the best ears on the farm, not counting Lester."

It was true that Cesar had heard everything—all the stops and starts, the highs and lows, even the first croak. But even better than his sense of hearing were his good manners. "I couldn't tell the difference. I thought it was Magellan," he said kindly.

"Really?" Gallileon asked. "It was really just the same?"

"Well," Cesar admitted, "you do have your own style, of course."

Gallileon groaned.

"But if you do the same at noon," said Cesar, "you will be fine. In fact, you will do even better now that you've had practice."

"I guess so," said Gallileon. He sat down and tried to collect his thoughts.

"Why don't you have a drink of water?" Cesar said gently. "It would be good for your voice."

"Yeah, you're probably right," said Gallileon. Then he noticed something. "Hey!" he cried. "Where's Pepina?"

Chapter 11

Secret Agent Pepina

Pepina had a funny feeling about Prattle, so she decided to follow him. As the ducks fell into formation, she snuck into the middle of the diamond. She was small, way below eye level, and with all the noise they were making with their big webbed feet and horrible laughter, she figured there was no way they would ever hear her. If they were up to something, she would find out and tell Gallileon. And when Pepina made up her mind, she always followed through, even if it seemed difficult or just plain silly.

First they came to the duck side of the pond. "Tell the others," barked Prattle. "We don't have much time."

"Time for what, boss?" asked Dip.

"It's almost noon already, you dimwit," snapped Prattle, "which means I don't have time to tell you my plan, which means you should just do what I say and not ask silly questions!"

The ducks scattered quickly, running for cover from Prattle's whiplike tongue. They quacked a gathering call to the female ducks, who tended to stay in the pond. Prattle waddled on hastily, almost too fast for Pepina to keep up. Ahead of them, through Prattle's bumpy legs, she could barely see the goose hideout. He honked loudly, and two geese in the distance began moving to greet him. Pepina hid behind a large stone, and none too soon. Prattle turned around, looking this way and that to make sure no one could hear them.

Babble and Gabble, the other two geese, arrived. "Where have you been?" asked Babble.

"And what's the hurry?" asked Gabble.

"Big news," said Prattle, "but I don't have much time to explain, so listen carefully."

The other geese hushed right away. They could hardly believe their good fortune to have *big news* two days in a row.

"Do you remember what the cat, what's his name, told us this morning?" asked Prattle.

"You mean Eli?" asked Babble.

"Yeah, that's his name," said Gabble. "He spouted off some nonsense about big lips is all I remember.

Whatever it was, it certainly wasn't worth the prize fish I caught for him."

"Oh yes, it was," said Prattle. "It was worth ten fish, at least. How else would we have known about what's happening today?"

"You mean the fair?" asked Gabble.

"Weren't you paying attention, blockhead?" hissed Prattle. "Look, I don't have time to explain this to you. So let me just tell you what happened while I was out."

"I know! We're going to tell everyone about the eek lapse, aren't we?" shouted Babble, honking with glee.

"No, you moron, we're not going to tell anyone about the *egg lips,*" said Prattle angrily. "That would spoil the plan."

I knew it! thought Pepina. *They're up to something.*

"What plan?" asked Gabble.

Prattle yelled in frustration, "The one I'm never going to have a chance to tell you if you keep interrupting!"

They fell silent.

"Now, if you can remember past what you ate for breakfast, then you'll recall that yesterday we delivered the news about Magellan, the feathery poofball the farmer is showing off at the fair."

Pepina almost cried out at their two-faced mention of her father.

Prattle continued, "Well, Magellan has a son, named Gallileon."

"Is he going to the fair, too?" asked Babble.

Prattle turned to her, speaking sweetly, as if to a child. "No, darling, he's not. Because if he were, he would be there already, wouldn't he?" Then Prattle smacked her on the side of the head with his wing. "Bozo! Now, for the last time, be quiet and listen!"

Pepina had to hold her beak shut to keep from laughing out loud. What buffoons these geese were!

Prattle continued while Babble rubbed her head. "Today Gallileon was the one making all that ruckus at dawn. He thinks he's grown-up enough to call the sun. As if the sun wouldn't rise anyway without those silly roosters. Anyway, he is giving a demonstration at noon to show everyone just how he did it."

"And we're going to tell everyone!" shouted Gabble.

"No, we're *not*!" Prattle screeched. He looked ready to throw a fit. "Oh, wait—yes, that we will do. We have to make sure everyone is watching; otherwise the plan will be useless."

"What plan?" asked Babble, moving back a safe distance in case Prattle decided to hit her again.

"Never mind. You are all hopeless," sighed Prattle. "Just get moving. You'll find out when everyone else does."

Pepina gulped. This was terrible. She wasn't sure exactly what Prattle had in mind, but she could tell they meant to trick Gallileon. She had to warn him, especially because whatever happened would be partly her fault. If something bad happened because of what she'd said, she wouldn't blame Gallileon if he never played with her again. Usually she wouldn't care about that, but today something had changed. For the first time, there were a few moments when she had actually *liked* her brother and had even felt proud of him . . . and now her big mouth had betrayed him to the enemy. But these geese had no idea who they were dealing with. *This means war!* she thought.

Then she screamed. Suddenly, without any warning, Pepina found herself two feet high in the air in a wet and smelly place.

"Hey, whoosh thish?" asked Wade with her mouth full of a kicking and hollering Pepina. Wade was the first duck to come and join the geese in their hideout.

Prattle turned and smiled. "Why, here's my good friend Pepina! What are you doing in goose territory, my dear? Are you thinking about joining us?"

"No way!" she yelled.

"Oh, then that means you're a spy. Well, you can hardly expect a warm welcome, then."

"Let me go!" cried Pepina, wiggling like a worm in Wade's beak.

"I don't think so," laughed Prattle. "What, so you can run to your precious brother? I don't know why you bother. He doesn't even like you!"

"You can't eat me," Pepina squealed, kicking her feet. "Everyone would come looking for me."

"I doubt that," snickered Prattle. "Hardly anyone even knows you exist. I bet the other animals don't even talk to you. With the exception of Cesar, of course, who is desperate for a friend."

"How would you know?" Pepina yelled. "Put me down," she demanded. "It smells in here!"

Prattle laughed and moved forward until Pepina was a mere inch away from one of his dark, glistening eyes. "Let's strike a deal, Pepina," he said. "We'll have Wade here put you down if you promise not to say a word until Gallileon has completed his . . . demo." He shushed her before she could say a thing. "It's up to you whether you want to witness history from inside Wade's beak or comfortably on the ground."

"How dare you!" Pepina yelled. She kicked and squirmed as hard as she could, but it made no difference. Finally, she gave up struggling. "Fine," she agreed sullenly. "I'll keep quiet. Now put me down!"

"That's more like it," said Prattle. He pulled her out of Wade's mouth and laid her softly on her feet. "You should think of us as your friends, Pepina," he said cheerfully. "We like you, 'cause you're an animal with pluck. True courage is a rare quality and is to be admired. Perhaps we can even be allies."

Pepina glared at him, her beak buttoned tight.

Prattle turned to his fellow geese and the six ducks that had gathered around. "Now, let's march!" he commanded. With Prattle in the lead, Pepina in between the two geese behind him, and the ducks following after in two rows of three, they set off.

Chapter 12

Showtime!

allileon watched as the geese, with six ducks behind them, paraded around the well in a large circle. They passed by each of the animals in turn while Prattle called, "Look one, look all, for a glimpse of true magic! This amazing ability has been preserved by roosters for generations. Now, for the first time, see with your very own eyes exactly how they do it! At noon the show begins! Stay tuned for the sun summoner, Gallileon the Great!"

Gallileon was still standing near Cesar's pen. Each time Prattle and his crew said his name, Gallileon felt like he was going to be ill. Cesar sat quietly, having run out of polite things to say.

Around and around the geese and ducks went as the sun crawled higher in the sky and heads popped out from every pen. Everyone was watching except

Lester, who was curled up at Mrs. Rosa's feet inside the house, and the chickens, who were taking a nap in the henhouse. Gallileon looked over to the chicken yard, grateful that they were nowhere in sight, though he thought Pepina would have explained what was going on by now.

Suddenly, a white head with squinty black eyes appeared before him. "Iiiiit's showtime!" Prattle shouted, looking as close to happy as he ever got. "C'mon, wonderboy, this is your big break!" he said, smiling broadly. "And in case you're having doubts, my dear," he added with the familiar wicked glint in his eyes, "one way or another, you will be the star of the show. So, whether it be as Gallileon the Great or as a fake and a fool, take your pick—but be quick."

Gallileon stood up slowly. "Good luck," whispered Cesar. He watched helplessly as Gallileon, wings slumped, dragged himself toward the well.

"Go up there," ordered Prattle, pointing his wing toward the roof on top of the well, "so everyone can hear you."

Gallileon was aware of the geese and ducks crowding close, but he felt too sick to pay any attention to them. He took a deep breath and jumped up, flapping like crazy, barely making it onto the first beam. For a moment, it felt like he might fall into the black, cool hole. The thought of falling woke him up a little, although, at the moment, it didn't seem like too bad an idea. He dug his claws deep into the wood. Then, with a gasp, he sprang outward and pulled himself onto the roof.

All eyes were on him. For the first time ever, he wished Lester would show up and make everyone go back to their business. At this point, Gallileon didn't care if he was a nobody on the farm or if he had to admit he wasn't grown-up yet. *If this is what being grown-up is like,* he thought, *I'd rather sleep on a haystack.*

From what seemed like miles away, Gallileon could hear Prattle's horrible nasal voice. "Ladies and gentlemen," he cried, "ponies and cows, chickens and goats, donkeys and sheep, ducks and geese, thank you for your attention! Today we are honored to present to you an unsung hero among us, a ruby-feathered wonder, son of the esteemed Magellan— the gallant sun summoner, Gallileon!"

The ducks and geese cheered while the other animals looked at one another with puzzled faces.

Prattle raised his voice to a screech. "Today, my friends, we will witness not *what* he does, for that we know already—he calls the sun, that marvelous sun, which makes the plants grow, gives us light, keeps us warm—but rather *how* he does it. And now," he boomed, "without further ado, we are pleased to present to you, the rrrrrrrrooster of the hour, Gallileon!"

A hush fell over the yard. The young rooster stood as tall as his trembling body would allow him. The midday sun was beating down on him like a hot hammer, as though angry with him, making him dizzy and weak. Gallileon cleared his throat, shook out his feathers, and tried to look confident. He raised his beak to the sky. He had to close his eyes to keep from being blinded. He drew in a long, deep breath, ignoring the pain in his throat and the tightness in his chest. Then, gathering all the anger, fear, courage, love, and joy he could find inside himself, he packed them all into a bundle and sent it flying into the air on an enormous note.

It was as if a wall had been broken. Deep, heartfelt crows poured out of him, sending him soaring up into the world of clouds. Suddenly, he was as free as a bit of dandelion puff on the breeze. He found himself growing, stretching outward to cover the entire sky. A tingle spread through his body like a flame. In an instant, Gallileon realized that he was gigantic, and he was on fire! He was no longer an

awkward rooster on top of a well—he was the sun!
He was king of the sky. He crowed and crowed, and
the world swayed beneath him.

Then he looked up. The sky seemed strange.
Something was missing. He shrank back into his
skin with a terrible sinking feeling. Where the brilliant midday sun had been moments before, there
was now a strange dark blotch. It was still the shape
of a circle, but rather than anything solid, it looked
like a hole through which the sun had escaped.

Showtime!

Fearfully, Gallileon glanced down at the scene below him. All of the animals had their eyes on that same hole. Even Mrs. Rosa, with Lester by her side, was gazing upward with one hand over her eyes. For the first time ever, Lester looked confused.

This was all wrong—very, very wrong. Gallileon couldn't believe his eyes. A moment ago he had been soaring through the sky, and now he was staring into a noontime twilight. Had he confused the sun by crowing at an unusual time and made it

think it was time to set? Or had he angered the sun by fooling with something he shouldn't have?

Prattle, never one to miss a dramatic moment, broke the silence. "Oh heavens!" he cried, running back and forth. "Spare us! What has Gallileon done? Is the sun angry with us now? What kind of rooster sings the sun into going? Is this some kind of joke? What do you have to say for yourself, Gallileon? What does the sun stealer have to say?"

The geese and ducks, as if on cue, turned toward the well. The other animals, who had no idea what to think, also turned. But no one answered the goose's challenge. Under the darkening sky, the well stood bare and silent. Gallileon was gone.

Chapter 13

Held Captive

Without warning, something grabbed Pepina, holding her sideways. Dip turned to her and hissed, "Nip has you. Now keep quiet or we will ruin your brother. It won't be hard, now that he's stolen the sun!"

Pepina blinked back tears. Nip had her gripped tightly in his beak, and she couldn't move anything except her head and toes. The other animals, who were all looking at each other in confusion and bombarding Lester with questions, never once noticed her. Pepina squirmed helplessly, watching her mother peer through the chicken wire, searching the crowd for her son and daughter. As the duck set off for the pond, she saw the sun disappear along with her chances of escape.

Nip took her for a long journey, past the farmer's house, along the vegetable patch, and then for a ride through the pond. The ride was bumpy and uncomfortable and stank of fish. When they finally arrived at the goose hideout, a group of rocks surrounded by bushes, all the geese and ducks were already there. By then the sun was back in its normal place, as if nothing strange had happened. Pepina wondered if she had just imagined it had disappeared.

Nip dropped her on a pile of dried leaves as the geese gathered around. "Welcome back, my dear," said Prattle. He turned to the ducks. "You!" he shouted. "Dip and Flip. Go and keep watch at the east side of the pond. Wade, Waddle, and Paddle, you can go home and inform us if anyone is coming. Nip, you stay here. Everybody got it? Now scram!" The ducks, except for Nip, all scurried off.

Pepina sneezed. She lay on the leaves like a limp rag doll, shaken and soggy. "Nip," growled Prattle, "what have you done with her? She's half-drowned!"

"You said to take her the long way back, boss," said Nip, "and it ain't like I have pockets or somethin'!"

"You took a shortcut through the pond, didn't you?" said Prattle. Nip looked at him fearfully. "You're a clumsy oaf!" Prattle shouted. "Entirely unfit to be my first officer!"

"What do you mean?" argued Nip. "Since when do we worry so much about prisoners?"

"That does it!" snapped Prattle. "From this moment on, you are now a lowly guard. Pepina is no prisoner, you idiot; she's our new member."

Pepina got up slowly. What on earth was going on? Did Prattle just say what she thought he'd said?

Prattle pointed to a spot past the bushes. "Go and keep watch on the lookout rock," he barked. "You've done enough damage here." Nip made a sound as if to speak, then stamped off angrily, muttering under his breath.

Prattle turned with a giant grin that looked as if it had been glued on. "So good to have you back, Pepina!" he said, trying his best to sound kind and friendly. "Make yourself at home! In fact, please consider this your new home. Right, ladies?" Babble and Gabble nodded and honked happily.

Pepina was too shocked and tired to be her usual feisty self. "What?" she asked weakly, slumping against a stone.

"Oh come, my dear," Prattle said. "You must know by now that you can't go back to your normal way of life, to your family—you're a traitor. They won't want you. And if Gallileon wouldn't play with you before, he won't even want to see you now that you've made him the laughingstock of the farm."

Pepina stared at him blankly, her heart sinking.

"But *we* like you," said Babble. "We'll be your friends and family. We think you're smart, too smart to waste your life growing up to be a hen who does nothing but sit around and lay eggs."

"Plus you've got style," added Gabble. "That's a great bow you have. You're the only animal on this farm with any fashion sense."

"Yes, my girl, you've got talent," said Prattle, still wearing that awful grin. "You've got pizzazz. So we've agreed to save you from what would be a sad fate indeed. Before the world can reject you and break your spirit, we'll take you in, give you a home, and give you a future. As a goose!"

Pepina's beak dropped open. "As a what?" she croaked.

"Quick," shouted Prattle, "she's going to pass out! Fetch a strip of algae! Make her a bed!"

Bustling around, the geese set about taking care of their guest. They were too busy to see the flicker of green eyes in the bushes or hear the swish of branches as a dark figure sprang out and padded softly toward the garden.

Chapter 14

Talking Shadows

Jolted by the sound of Prattle's voice when the sun had disappeared, Gallileon took action. Before he realized what he was doing, he leapt from the well and began to run. His feet led him away from the crowd and past Cesar's pen, and then he took a sharp left down a stone path. Finally, Gallileon could run no farther. He leaned against a thin tree trunk and sank to the ground. Blinking and gasping, he looked around. He had wound up in one of his favorite hiding places, a small grove of lime trees.

Gallileon's head was spinning. He stared into space, dazed. Nothing made sense. What had happened to the sun? Was it his fault? Was the sun really angry? Did he have some strange power that he didn't know how to control? If so, maybe he should never crow again.

The only solution he saw was to run away. If he couldn't do the one thing that made roosters useful, he didn't deserve to stay on the farm. Gallileon looked around at the lime trees. He would miss this spot more than any other. And of course he would miss his family terribly, even Pepina. *But they can get along without me,* he thought. He realized, with a pang of guilt, that he had hardly spent any time with them. Usually he went off on his own as soon as he woke and only came home at night to eat and sleep. *Prattle was right,* he thought sadly. *I am useless.*

Gallileon sat gloomily among the lime trees, staring into the shadows and trying to build up the nerve to take that first step away from home. At some point, he got the feeling that one of the shadows was watching him. Presently it spoke. "Good afternoon," it said in a soft voice.

Gallileon wasn't in the mood for surprises, so even talking shadows didn't startle him. The voice sounded familiar, but he didn't feel like being polite, so he ignored it.

Two emerald eyes shone out from the speaking bush. "What's the matter? Cat got your tongue?" asked the voice, chuckling dryly.

In a flash, Gallileon recognized Eli, whom everyone called "the witch's cat." Leila had warned him not to get mixed up with Eli, as he was supposed to bring bad luck. At the moment, Gallileon didn't think his luck could be much worse. But he didn't feel like talking.

Eli stepped out from inside the bush and stretched his sleek black body. He took five steps toward Gallileon, then curled up comfortably in front of him. "Excuse me for jesting," said the cat. "It is a bit rude. But it is not like you to be so silent, Gallileon," he said. "If it weren't for what I saw today, I might think you were afraid of me, like all the others. But from what I saw at the well, it is clear that you are a rooster of great courage."

"Courage? Ha," scoffed Gallileon. "Foolishness, maybe, but hardly courage."

"As you like," replied Eli. "But neither courage nor foolishness is a crime, so what troubles you?"

"Well, if you've seen all that happened today, you should know," said Gallileon sourly.

"I never assume anything," said Eli, licking his paws thoughtfully.

"Sorry, but I can't talk about it," said Gallileon. "I've never been more confused in my entire life. So don't expect me to have any answers."

Rooster and cat sat in silence for a few slow-moving minutes. Neither so much as twitched a

feather or a whisker. Then Gallileon, who had been puzzling over it for some time, burst out, "I just don't understand how the sun could disappear like that!" He kicked a small stone. "Was it me?" he asked angrily. "Was it my fault? Maybe the sun thought I was trying to show off, so it went away. Or maybe it got confused."

"Would it help to know that the sun is back?" asked Eli.

"What?" Gallileon cried, looking up sharply. Sure enough, the sun was back up in the sky, exactly where it was supposed to be. Under the shade of the lime trees, he had failed to notice. For a second, he thought about just going home, eating lunch, and letting Leila explain everything to him. But that would be babyish, he thought. He was too old now to be running back to his parents every time he had a problem. He would have to solve this one for himself. "I don't know," Gallileon muttered. "I don't know anything anymore."

"That's a good place to begin," said Eli. "Before one can learn anything, one first has to admit one knows nothing."

"You really *are* a witch's cat, aren't you?" accused Gallileon.

"What makes you think that?" asked Eli, trying not to laugh.

"You talk weird," Gallileon said.

Eli broke into a smile. "Well, you sing weird."

Gallileon frowned.

"It's a joke," Eli said. "No need to take things so personal." He grinned, his eyes sparkling with laughter. "Anyway, even if I *were* a witch's cat," he purred, "what would that have to do with you? What makes a witch's cat different from any other cat?"

"You're black," said Gallileon.

"And you're red," said Eli. "So what?"

"But don't you fetch ingredients for spells and potions and things?" asked Gallileon.

"What do I look like, a servant?" said Eli, twitching his tail with annoyance. "And even if I did, there aren't any witches around here, so why would it matter?"

Gallileon thought about that. In a few moments, he had what he thought was a witty reply. "It's not what you do that frightens the other animals," he said, "it's what you know. Don't you know about magic and stuff?"

Eli's eyes flashed. "Ah! Now you're getting closer," he said. "But you've got it backwards. The danger is not what people know but what they do with their knowledge. I do happen to be in the business of information. All that means is that I sit, watch, and listen to whatever goes on around me. Sometimes what I find out comes in handy later, either for me or for someone else. But that is not witchcraft; it is simply being observant. Magic is a whole other matter."

Now Gallileon understood why Eli was rarely seen. It was because he kept quiet, listening and watching. Gallileon was usually so wrapped up in his thoughts, he noticed very little. There were many days he had missed supper because he had stayed out past sunset, daydreaming. "That sounds like a good skill to have," said Gallileon.

Eli looked pleased. "Well, it's not something you're born with. It has to be learned. But anyone can do it."

"Not me," said Gallileon. "I think too much."

"I bet you could if you tried," said Eli. "Why don't we try a little experiment?"

"Okay," agreed Gallileon, his curiosity making him forget his troubles. "Why not?"

Eli stood and began walking in circles around Gallileon. "Don't look at me," he said. "Close your eyes. What I want you to do is stand still and focus on what you hear. Ready?"

"Yes," said Gallileon, who was having a hard time keeping his balance with his eyes shut. At first it was hard to pay attention. His mind wanted to wander. *This is silly,* he thought. But then he noticed that it seemed the breeze was a little sharper than before. His body tingled all over, as if he had been half-sleeping and was only now fully awake. He smelled corn cooking. His stomach started to growl. He heard grass blades bending under Eli's paws and the *kerthunk* of a lime falling from a tree. In the distance, he could hear Mrs. Rosa calling for Lester, and the funny snuffling sounds he made whenever she gave him something good to eat. Everything seemed much more alive than before!

"All right," Eli said suddenly, "what did you hear?"

Gallileon tried to recall what he had observed. "I heard you walking, for a start," he said. "Then a lime fell, and Lester got a treat."

"Lucky dog," said Eli. "Well, that's a good start. Did you notice anything else?"

"Sure," said Gallileon. "The wind on my feathers and the smell of corn cooking. I'm hungry!"

Eli winked. "See, you're getting the hang of it pretty fast. All it takes is a certain kind of focus. I'm glad you're so naturally observant, because it's a skill you're going to need if you want to find out what happened to the sun today."

"What do you mean?" asked Gallileon. "Do I just shut my eyes?"

"Not exactly," he said, taking a step forward. "We're going to go for a walk."

Gallileon paused. He would never be able to slip away quietly if he was with Eli. Then again, he was not so sure he still wanted to leave the farm. Maybe if he found out what had really happened to the sun, he wouldn't have to go! As Gallileon began to follow Eli through the grass, he had a strange thought. "Did the sun go away because of some sort of magic?"

Instead of answering, Eli just smiled.

Chapter 15

The Fashion Show

Pepina opened her eyes. Something like a green towel was draped over her face. It was cold and slimy. She was just about to fling it off and sit up when she heard Prattle's voice close by.

"She should be waking up any moment now," Prattle said.

Pepina lay still. She figured it was probably better to let them think she was asleep.

"What if she doesn't want to stay here with us?" asked Babble.

"Or if someone comes looking for her?" added Gabble.

Prattle sounded annoyed. "First of all," he said, "she doesn't have a choice about whether she stays or not. If she starts making a scene, we'll just leave her on a lily pad in the center of the pond. Only ducks and geese can swim, so no one would ever find her there. So, if she knows what's best for her, she'll join us without a fuss."

Pepina thought she might faint again. This was even worse than she had thought. The idea of being left alone, stranded in the middle of the pond, was more horrible than anything she could ever imagine. She decided to be on her best behavior with the geese, no matter how angry they made her. It was her only chance of ever getting away from them.

"As for what to do about intruders," Prattle continued, "we've got six ducks standing guard on both sides of the pond. If anyone comes looking, we'll have plenty of time to hide her. But I think Pepina's smart enough to know it's pointless to resist. In fact, she's probably listening right now. Let's have a look, shall we?" He walked over and peeled the pond scum from Pepina's face.

Pepina pretended to be fast asleep.

"Very clever," said Prattle. "But the sooner you open your eyes, the sooner you can dry off so you don't catch cold. Or," he continued, with a mischievous tone, "maybe we should dunk her in the pond to make sure she's okay."

When she heard the other geese's footsteps, Pepina slowly stretched and opened her eyes. She shuddered at the thought of being hidden until everyone had given up looking for her. She would have to be very careful.

"W-what happened?" she said as if she had just woken up. "What's this green stuff? And why am I so cold?"

"Why, hello," Prattle greeted her warmly. "I'm afraid you caught a fright earlier and passed out. The algae was to help bring you around. I'm glad to see it has worked. Why don't we dry you off? You must be freezing, you poor thing!"

Babble stepped forward holding a bit of yellow cloth. She seemed unsure of what to do with it. She paused, then dropped it in front of Pepina.

"Not like that!" snapped Prattle, picking it up in his beak. Carefully, as if tending to his own child, he draped it around Pepina like a blanket.

"My, doesn't she look cute!" exclaimed Gabble.

"She certainly does," agreed Babble.

"It's like having our very own gosling!" cried Gabble.

"Yes, and I've always wanted a little doll to play dress-up with," said Babble.

Pepina looked at them blankly. Inside, she was boiling with rage, but she knew that to show it would be risky. Instead, she put on her most innocent face and asked, "Don't you have any young of your own?"

"No," Gabble replied sadly. "We've always wanted one, though."

"Maybe Pepina would like to be our adopted child!" said Babble.

"What a great idea," Prattle said. "You would love that, wouldn't you, Pepina?"

Pepina felt like saying that she would rather eat moldy corn and that she already had a mother and father. But then she thought better of it, gritted her beak, and said with as much cheerfulness as she could fake, "Oh yes, I'd love that! If I went home now, my family would probably throw me out for helping you make a fool of my brother. So it's best if I stay with you."

Babble and Gabble were delighted. They flapped their wings and honked with glee. Prattle simply grinned smugly. "A very wise decision," he said. "But how can we be sure you mean it?"

Pepina's eyes flashed. She smiled sweetly and asked, "Don't you trust my word?"

Prattle took a step closer. "Of course we are glad you have the good sense to choose a life with us," he said, "but, unfortunately, words mean very little. You have to leave your old and rather sad little life as a baby chicken behind before beginning a new and better one with us."

Pepina tried not to show her annoyance. "How am I supposed to . . . I mean, how does one do that?" she asked.

"Good question," Prattle replied. "Well, it would be difficult for us to make you look like a goose or a gosling. You're too small and fluffy, and your feathers are yellow. However, we can help you to look less like yourself."

"What do you mean?" asked Pepina, feeling frightened.

Prattle broke out into his thin, nasal laughter. "Don't worry, my dear," he said. "We'll figure out a way. But first of all, we'll need to get rid of this." In one quick motion, like a snake striking its prey, Prattle snapped down and removed Pepina's favorite bow from around her neck.

"Hey! That's mine!" Pepina yelled, unable to hide her anger. She threw off the yellow cloth and hopped up, trying to reach her bow, which was dangling from Prattle's beak. He passed it to Babble, who danced around with it proudly.

Prattle grabbed Pepina and forced her to sit down. "Calm down, my little hothead. We haven't stolen it," he said. "That would hardly be very friendly of us, would it? With that bow, anyone would know you from a distance, so we have to keep it safe for a while. We can give you other, even better things to wear in return. Can't we, girls?"

Gabble nodded. "Shall I fetch the box?" she asked eagerly.

"That's a good idea," said Prattle. "We can have a little fashion show!"

"A fashion show!" cried Babble, dropping the bow in her excitement. "What fun!"

Pepina took a deep breath, trying to prepare herself for whatever it was they were planning. It didn't sound anything like fun, but it was better than being stranded on a lily pad in the middle of the pond.

Gabble returned with a rusty cigar tin in her beak. She flung it on the ground and it popped open. Dirty rings, bits of string, and other strange objects rolled out onto the ground She gazed at them fondly.

"This is our treasure chest," boasted Babble.

Pepina was speechless. What in the world were they planning to do? It looked like a bunch of junk—scraps of cloth, bits of trash, and old, thrown-out jewelry. Did they really expect her to be impressed?

"See how generous we are?" said Prattle. "You

lend us your bow, and we give you all this to wear—a whole year's worth of collecting!"

Pepina shuddered. *There's no way I'm going to put on any of that garbage,* she thought. But before she could think of a way to talk them out of it, Gabble took an old, yellowed cloth and tossed it over Pepina's head. The rag, which had once been a fancy napkin, had a large hole in it and fit like a lopsided poncho. "I found this near the farmer's house!" Gabble boasted. "It's my favorite piece of cloth."

Next came the anklets. Babble dug around in the tin box and pulled out a ring. "Here's one I found near the pond!" she sang. Pepina frowned. It was old and worn with a large plastic ruby. Gabble pulled out another, a thin, bent ring with a little metal heart. "Oh, she'll look darling in this!" exclaimed Gabble. The geese made Pepina step through the rings so she had bangles on either leg that slipped down and rested on top of her feet.

"Now we need a belt!" said Babble. She hunted in the little box and returned with a bit of tangled string. Prattle lost his patience more than once while Babble and Gabble tried to work out whose end should go under and whose should go over. They finally managed to tie it loosely around Pepina's middle. Pepina looked down at the mass of knots and tangles that hung down around her like a net.

"Oh, doesn't she look adorable!" Gabble cooed. Pepina was glad she didn't have a mirror.

Finally, Babble added the finishing touch: A shiny aluminum bag from a long-gone packet of cookies became a hat. "And here's a crown for the princess!" Babble bubbled. The bag-hat was too big and slipped down over Pepina's eyes.

"My goodness, Pepina!" cried Babble. "You look like a star!"

"Indeed you do," agreed Gabble. "What a gorgeous little gosling you'll make!"

Prattle adjusted the hat and smoothed out the dress with his beak. "Not bad," he said, looking pleased. "You wouldn't even recognize yourself in this getup. Good work, geese!" he said. "Very nice indeed! Why don't you turn around, Pepina, so we can see how it looks on all sides?"

Pepina looked at the geese, then looked down at the rings. Slowly she turned around, then tried walking. After three careful steps, she stumbled and fell. Babble picked Pepina up and set her back on her feet. "Oops!" Gabble said cheerily. "I guess that's the price of being fashionable."

Pepina looked down at the ground. She felt ridiculous in this strange outfit, and she was still upset about the bow. She stretched her wings, which were covered by the yellowed cloth. Then the bag fell back over her eyes. As she stared into the darkness, waiting for someone to lift it back up, she felt like a ticking time bomb. It was only a matter of minutes before she could no longer hold her feelings in. Pepina was just about ready to explode.

Chapter 16

Gallileon Goes Hunting

"**W**here are we going?" asked Gallileon, who was still following Eli through the grass.

"We're going hunting," Eli replied.

"Hunting for what?" asked Gallileon. "I only eat bugs and corn. I would never eat a mouse." He made a face at the thought. "Ugh!"

"Nor would I," agreed Eli. "I prefer fish. But anyway, we're not looking for food. We're gathering information."

"Really?" asked Gallileon. "How do we do that?"

Eli turned around and looked Gallileon in the eye. He lowered his voice to make his point clear. "The first step," he said firmly, "involves being completely silent. So instead of thinking about what we're looking for and coming up with all sorts of silly questions, focus on listening to our surroundings and finding your answers there." He turned and continued walking.

Gallileon felt foolish. Why did he always have to talk? But walking with someone in silence felt weird, and trying not to think about anything was even stranger. Still, the cat looked like he knew what he was doing, and Eli had a certain grace that Gallileon longed to have. So they walked without speaking, and after a while, Gallileon knew where they were heading. A glint of blue shimmered through the leaves.

"Hey!" he whispered. "That's the fishpond!"

Eli just nodded.

"But we might get caught!" said Gallileon nervously. "Ducks don't like roosters."

"That's precisely why we have to be quiet," growled Eli.

"But what are we looking for? What's the point?" protested Gallileon, who was afraid of being so close to enemy territory.

Eli stared at him. "Do you want to find out what happened to the sun or not?" he asked.

"Yes, of course I do," replied Gallileon, "but—"

Eli interrupted. "Then you'll have to trust me. And you'll also have to trust yourself. But whatever you do, be observant!"

Gallileon nodded, blushing. *What am I?* he thought. *Chicken?* Then his side began to itch, just under the left wing. He tried to ignore it, but the itch grew and grew until the only thing he could think about was scratching it. He peeked over to see if Eli was watching, then bent down and nipped it. "Ahhhhh," he sighed.

Eli gave him a stern look. "It's safe," he said. "Let's go."

Carefully and quietly, they moved forward, bush by bush. Every so often, Eli would stop and listen, whiskers pointing straight out to pick up signs of danger. At one point, Gallileon thought he heard something. Eli peered curiously out from the bushes. Gallileon could barely keep himself from shouting out what was already obvious: Two ducks were coming!

Soon they appeared, waddling noisily down the path. Gallileon recognized them immediately. It was Dip and Flip. *But where is Nip?* Gallileon wondered.

"Watch duty, watch duty," Dip complained. "We always get stuck with boring old watch duty!"

"Yeah," said Flip, "unlike Nip, the boss's favorite."

"That's because he wants to be a boss, like Prattle," said Dip.

"Well, good for him," said Flip. "I wouldn't want to hang out with Prattle all the time, anyhow."

Dip laughed. "Me neither," he cried. "Wade, Waddle, and Paddle are the real lucky ones—they get to stay home and play all day. They never have to be at Prattle's beck and call."

"That's because they're girls," said Flip. "They're not interested in being soldiers."

"Well, sometimes I wonder what the big deal is," said Dip. "Being a soldier is no fun if all we do is patrol the pond for the geese."

"But that's *not* all we do," reminded Flip. "Today we were part of that big mission with the rooster."

"Oh yeah!" laughed Dip. "Hey, did you see the look on his face when he saw that the sun was gone?"

Gallileon gasped. Eli gave him a warning look.

"Actually, I didn't," said Flip. "I was too busy trying not to be trampled by that scaredy-pig. Did you?"

Dip paused. "Well, no," he said. "But I bet it was funny!" Both ducks giggled and quacked with glee.

"Hey!" said Flip, giving Dip a playful shove. "I have an idea!"

Dip pushed him back. "What is it?" he asked.

"Why don't we keep watch for intruders that

might be coming up from inside the pond?" laughed Flip. "Then we could do our job and have a nice swim at the same time."

"That's the best idea I've heard all day!" cried Dip. "Why don't we make you boss?"

"Yeah!" shouted Flip. "You should. Because if I were boss, this is what I'd say: Last one in is a rotten egg!" Laughing and quacking, the two ducks ran toward the water and dove in. Then they began a splashing contest.

Eli nudged Gallileon, who was in a daze. They ran down the path until they were well out of sight, then slowed down to a careful walk.

Gallileon turned to Eli with a question on his beak, but Eli stopped him short. "We're gathering information," Eli said. "There's no point in saying anything until we have something to discuss."

Chapter 17

The Secret Word

Gallileon and Eli followed the bushes along the dirt path by the pond. Every now and then, Eli would stop and sniff, or stand as still as a statue, testing the air with his whiskers. Gallileon still had no clue what they were looking for, but he had a growing feeling that it was going to explain exactly what he needed to know.

After what he had seen with Dip and Flip, Gallileon realized how valuable a skill observation really was. It seemed to him that most people never paid much attention to their surroundings, even when they were supposed to be keeping watch! He felt like he had a special power, like a magic spell that made him invisible. After all, no goose could ever hurt him if it didn't know he was there!

Eli had stopped again. The path was curving

around the edge of the pond. "The geese live just down from this curve, among a group of rocks," said Eli softly. "And if they are home, they're bound to have guards. I'll scout ahead and check."

"Wait!" cried Gallileon. "You mean you've been here before?" he asked, surprised.

"I've been everywhere on the farm, and some places off it," Eli replied, jumping lightly onto the path. In a flicker, he was out of sight. Gallileon's heart was beating fast with a mixture of fear and excitement. He closed his eyes and breathed deeply to calm his nerves. He tried to expand his senses like he had before. But except for the sound of water gurgling among the rocks, he couldn't hear much at all.

When Gallileon opened his eyes, he was startled to find Eli's emerald eyes staring into his. He gasped in surprise.

"The second thing you must learn when it comes to observation," Eli said, "is to shut out the world without shutting your eyes. I have been standing here waiting for you to notice me for exactly two minutes and forty-three seconds."

Gallileon scratched nervously.

"Keep still!" Eli hissed. "Remember where you are! A single sneeze could give us away."

"Sorry," said Gallileon, stopping in mid-scratch.

"Don't be sorry," said Eli, giving him a friendly brush with his tail. "Just be careful. I won't be able to help you with this next part."

"Why not?" asked Gallileon.

"Because I have to be a decoy," said Eli. "There's another guard out there, a duck."

"It's probably Nip," said Gallileon. "The other ducks said he was with Prattle."

"Good thinking," said Eli. "It's useful to know his name."

Gallileon smiled, proud to have finally noticed something useful. "What's a decoy?" he asked.

"It's something that acts as a distraction. I'll get Nip's attention so that he won't notice you. But we need to form a plan," said Eli, "a strategy."

"Okay!" said Gallileon, excited. What had started off as an exercise was turning into a full-blown adventure!

"This is what we'll do," said Eli. "You can walk with me up to a certain point, where I'll have you wait. Then I'll go up and talk to the guard. With any luck, he'll follow me down to the vegetable patch. If he does, I'll call out a key word."

"A what?" asked Gallileon.

"A key word is something with a secret message

other than the plain meaning of the word," Eli said. He thought for a moment, twitching his whiskers. "The key word is *onward*," he said.

"Onward?" asked Gallileon. "That sounds pretty boring to me. It might as well be *strawberry*!"

"Well," said Eli, "if that sounds boring to you, keep in mind that it *has* to be perfectly ordinary so that no one suspects anything. But it still has to fit with the conversation, and I don't think ducks care much for strawberries."

He continued, "Now, after Nip follows me, you climb up to the rock where he has been standing, and observe."

"That's all?" asked Gallileon. "I just go up there? But what do I do after that?"

"That's up to you," said Eli. "I only lead others to information. I don't tell them what to do with it. But whatever you do, make sure you are not seen or heard yourself."

"But wait, Eli! Where will you be?" Gallileon asked. "You're not going to just leave me with the geese, are you?" Suddenly, Gallileon wondered if this was all some sort of trick.

Eli snorted, as if he had heard Gallileon's thoughts. "Either you trust me or you don't," said Eli gruffly. "If you do, then do as I say and follow after. If not, you're on your own. The most important thing is to trust yourself." With that, he began walking.

Gallileon hesitated. What was the right thing to do? Was Eli a friend or a foe? To walk boldly into goose territory seemed crazy. Especially to look for something he wasn't even sure he'd recognize if he saw it. Then again, deep down, Gallileon liked Eli. He wasn't warm and friendly like Cesar, but he still seemed like a friend.

A strong wave of curiosity made up Gallileon's mind for him. Whether Eli was on his side or not didn't really matter, he decided. With his new power, Gallileon felt like he could take care of himself.

Eli was almost out of sight. As quickly and as quietly as he could, Gallileon jumped out of the bushes and ran to catch up with him.

Chapter 18

Eli's Trick

ip paced back and forth angrily. He had been pacing ever since he reached the lookout rock. "Just what does that Prattle think I am?" he growled. "A slave? Just somebody to boss around and carry out his dirty work, while he doesn't even lift a feather?"

He turned to the rock, imagining it was Prattle. "Ha!" he spat. "Well, you're wrong about that! I'm not breaking my back for you anymore. I'm a duck, not a mule!"

Nip waddled even faster. "And what thanks do I get for all my hard work?" he shouted at the daisies and clover. "Nothing! Nada! No gratitude! Well, no more! His plans always stink, anyway. I'd make a much better boss than him."

"I agree," said a soft, calm voice.

Nip spun around. "A cat!" he hissed. "What are you doing here?"

Eli, who was sitting calmly in a patch of sunlight, gazed at Nip without blinking, then yawned slowly to show his fangs. "The name is Eli, my dear Nip."

Nip, who was getting ready to sound the alarm, stopped short. He was stunned. "How did you know my name?" he asked.

Eli smiled and began to inspect his sharp claws. "I know many things," he said. "I know, for instance, that your two duck friends are only pretending to patrol the pond. What they're really up to is enjoying a swim and talking about how glad they are not to be anywhere near Prattle."

Nip was all ears. "Really?" he asked.

Eli continued, "In fact, they were saying how much better things would be if you were the boss instead of him. And, judging from what I've seen, I very much agree."

"What do you mean?" asked Nip suspiciously. "What would you know about the business of ducks and geese?"

Eli began to groom himself, as if they were talking about peas and carrots. "For one, I know that Prattle is very lazy. He comes up with ideas but never does anything about them himself."

"That's just what I was saying!" said Nip.

"For two," continued Eli, licking his front paws, "Prattle doesn't have any friends. Even the other geese don't really like to be around him."

"That's because he's mean to everyone," said Nip.

"So," said Eli, "if they had a choice between Prattle and yourself, you might stand a decent chance." Eli grinned. "You're even better-looking," he joked.

Nip thought about it. The other geese never seemed to notice him. But at least they didn't dislike him. "Hmmmm," he said. "Maybe."

Eli stood up. He wasn't going to give Nip a chance to back down. "Listen," he hissed softly, "when you want to put a stop to a cold, mean boss like Prattle, you have to know his real weakness."

"Weakness?" Nip asked. "Prattle doesn't care about anything or anyone except himself. So what could possibly be his soft spot?"

"Exactly!" said Eli, taking a step forward. "Prattle is a coward," he added in a low voice. He moved closer and whispered, "Prattle is bigger and meaner than all of the small animals on the farm, so he doesn't have to be afraid of them. And because the cow, pony, sheep, goat, and donkey do not concern themselves with the business of birds, he doesn't

have to worry about them, either. There is only one animal on the farm he is really afraid of. So who does that leave?"

Nip thought hard. Seeing Eli's eyes glowing in the sun, he took a step back and asked, "You?"

Eli laughed silently. This wasn't the answer he expected, but it was even better to let the duck believe that. "Correct!" Eli said, trying to sound tough. "Haven't you seen the geese giving me a fish every morning as a toll?"

Nip gulped. Just this morning he had seen Gabble dive in the pond and bring out a beautiful fish, which she had then tossed toward a black shadow. Nip had been too busy running around carrying out Prattle's orders to pay close attention.

"So," continued Eli, "if you want to be the new boss of the pond, you'll have to listen to me." He inspected his claws again to make sure Nip understood.

"Okay," Nip squeaked.

"Here's the plan," said Eli. "First, we'll have to get some corn. I bet the geese haven't given Pepina any food, have they?"

"How . . . how did you know about the chick?" gasped Nip.

"I know many things!" snapped Eli. "We have to work fast, so listen up. Now, if you bring the corn to the chick, not only will it show the geese that you have thought of something Prattle hasn't, but it might also help Pepina to trust you a bit more."

"What has she got to do with anything?"

"Don't be so slow," said Eli. "If you want to challenge Prattle's rule, then you have to rebel against his orders. So if he says the chick has to stay, then what do you do?"

"I say the chick has to go!" shouted Nip.

"Exactly," said Eli. "You must also be extra polite and pleasant to the other geese. Flatter them. Make them like you. Meanwhile, I will find a way of dealing with Prattle."

"If he's so afraid of you," asked Nip, "then why can't you just go in and tell him to release the chick?"

"If I did that," Eli said, "how would that help you become the boss of the pond?"

"Well, that's true enough," said Nip. "But why do you care so much about me?"

Eli shook his head. "I'm tired of explaining everything to you. Let's just say that, like many others on the farm, I have a bone to pick with Prattle."

"I see," said Nip. "I can believe that."

"I should think so," said Eli. "Now, back to business. When Prattle runs away, the other geese will see what a coward he is and will accept you as the new leader." Eli flicked Nip with his tail. "Understand?"

"Wow, what a plan!" shouted Nip. "That's much better than anything Prattle ever came up with. Sure, count me in. I wasn't going to stay here twiddling my feathers around this stupid rock, anyway."

"Excellent," said Eli, turning toward the garden. "Then, *onward!*" Nip never noticed that Eli had raised his voice a great deal for that last word. He was too busy planning how to take over the pond.

Chapter 19

A Strange Creature

Gallileon had been waiting so long inside a bush, he was beginning to feel like he was turning into one. His legs felt wooden and heavy, and he was covered with leaves. He was just shaking out his feet, trying to get some life into them, when he heard Eli shouting, *"Onward!"*

That meant go! Gallileon crept out from the bush and inched slowly around the curve. He kept in the shadows whenever possible. Soon he could see the lookout rock Eli had pointed out. No one in sight. Step by step, he made his way closer.

There wasn't much to see. It was a large rock, with a good view of the path and the pond but no view of the geese's hideout. Gallileon hopped to the top and looked for Eli. He spotted him right away, a tiny black dot next to a small white dot. They were moving toward the garden.

He made himself comfortable on the stone and breathed deeply. *I mustn't close my eyes this time,* he thought. It was a little more difficult to focus on his sense of hearing with his eyes open, but slowly Gallileon was able to make out the different layers of sound. Soon he began to hear a tiny, high-pitched voice. It sounded angry. "Get me outta here!" it cried. "I'm sick of this! There's no way you can keep this up for long!"

Gallileon sat up straight and looked around. How strange! It sounded like a muffled mouse. He listened hard until he could make it out again. "Wait till Gallileon finds out about the trick you played on him," it said. "Then the whole farm will know what liars you are. They'll never trust any of your news again."

"I expect we shall be waiting a long time," replied a sharp, nasal voice. "How is he ever going to know if no one tells him? You certainly won't have the chance."

Gallileon gasped. So this is what Eli wanted him to find out! The geese had tricked him! But how? Surely they didn't have control over the sun? He had to find out more. Quietly, Gallileon began to climb down the slope that led to the pond. He moved at a crawl, inch by inch, until he was standing behind a tulip plant, with a good view of the goose hideout.

There they were! The long-necked Babble, the orange-nosed Gabble, and the beady-eyed Prattle. But who or what was *that*? In front of the geese stood, or rather wobbled, the strangest thing Gallileon had ever laid eyes on. At first he thought it was a pile of rags blowing in the breeze. But the air was still, and the creature, whatever it was, was now hopping up and down. It stuck out a thin, tiny leg and shook it, causing something to fly off and land in front of Babble.

Gallileon watched, curious, as Babble rushed over and snatched it up. Then another one came flying off, and Gabble chased after it, catching it right before it rolled into the pond. They picked up each object lovingly and placed them in a rusty tin box. Then they watched with looks of horror as a tangled piece of string fell to the ground like a broken fishnet. Gallileon strained his eyes to see what was underneath the yellowed poncho. It looked like something was struggling to get out.

Prattle sprang forward, digging the items back out of the box. He threw them at the creature. "Put them back on this instant!" he demanded.

The mystery animal screamed. It had a high-pitched, piercing voice. "Noooooooooo!" it shouted. "I refuse to wear this junk any longer!" It stamped its feet, and the shiny aluminum hat fell to the ground.

Gallileon almost cried out in shock when he saw who it was. *Pepina!* he yelled silently. *What in the world are those geese doing with you?*

Gallileon watched as Pepina threw off the rest of her costume.

"She doesn't want to wear her new clothes?" asked Babble.

"But why not?" whined Gabble. "She looked so pretty."

Gallileon heard voices behind him and looked up the hill to see where the sound was coming from. Nip and Eli had just returned to the lookout rock and were heading his way! He didn't have time to think about what to do. So he ran.

Chapter 20

A Friend in Need

Before he had any idea where he was going, Gallileon found himself at the well. He had run as if his feathers were on fire. He paused, taking in great gulps of air, and tried to figure out what he was going to do about saving Pepina. He couldn't tell his mother; she would be sick with worry. The other animals wouldn't want to leave their pens, and besides, they might tell Leila. There was no saying where Eli had gone, and Lester was almost impossible to talk to.

A cheerful voice broke into his thoughts. "Hi, Gallileon!" said Cesar. "Good to see you again!"

Gallileon turned, startled. He was still in "observation mode" and had forgotten that anyone could see him.

"Come in, come in," Cesar said warmly. "I was

just sitting down for a nibble, and I'd be happy to share it."

In the blink of an eye, Gallileon was up and over the fence and into Cesar's pen, hiding behind the trough. He didn't like the idea of being seen. After sneaking through the bushes for so long, he felt safer when he was out of view.

Cesar spread out a soft light-blue blanket and placed a couple of sugar biscuits down on top of it. "I saved these from lunch," he said proudly, "and now I'm doubly glad I did. Would you like something to drink?"

"Uhhhh . . . ," Gallileon said, trying to figure out how to break the news.

"I'll take that as a yes," said Cesar. He wondered why Gallileon seemed so jumpy. *Perhaps,* thought Cesar, *he is embarrassed by what happened this afternoon and doesn't want to talk about it with anyone.* Although he was burning with curiosity about what Gallileon thought about the sun, he decided not to bring it up. "Aren't you hungry?" asked Cesar hopefully.

"Not really," replied Gallileon, staring into space.

"Very well, then," sighed Cesar, joining him behind the trough. He had been greatly looking forward to his afternoon snack but knew it was rude to eat in front of others. To hide his disappointment, he took a dainty sip of water.

They sat awkwardly for a few moments. Gallileon was lost in thought, and Cesar was scolding himself for being such a bad host. Finally, Gallileon motioned for Cesar to come closer. Cesar stepped forward, trembling with a mixture of curiosity and worry. When Cesar had come within a few inches of Gallileon's beak, the rooster looked around nervously and said, "I have a big problem."

"You can tell me," said Cesar. "I am a good listener."

"I don't want Leila to find out. It's very important," Gallileon whispered.

"I'm very good at keeping secrets," Cesar insisted.

"Yes, and you might even be able to help," said Gallileon.

"Of course I will!" said Cesar. "I'll do anything for a friend."

"Well, here's the trouble. The geese have captured Pepina," he said. "I was just down at the pond and saw them all there."

"What?!" cried Cesar, jumping up into the air. His eyes grew wide with shock. "They have Pepina?"

"Shhhhh! Keep it down!" said Gallileon, looking

over the trough. "Somebody might hear us."

"Well, maybe they should!" replied Cesar, springing to the center of the pen. "I think everyone should!" He ran in circles, shouting, "This is an outrage! We must do something! Those geese have gone too far this time!" Around and around he went, kicking up a great cloud of dust. Finally, huffing and puffing, he fell in a heap on the blanket, completely spent.

Gallileon came to join him. *So much for trying to keep this quiet,* he thought. He walked over toward Cesar, stepping over the bits of food that had been knocked over during the pig's fit. The pen looked like it had been hit by a hurricane. Cesar had tripped over a large pile of goodies he had stashed away. Now the usually spotless floor was covered with popcorn, watermelon rinds, half an apple, and a handful of peanuts.

"Oh dear," sighed Cesar, looking down at the crumbs that had once been two lovely biscuits. "I do apologize," he said, blushing. "I don't know what came over me." The pig, who was covered in dust and had bits of food stuck to the bottoms of his feet, looked so sorry and ashamed about his outburst that Gallileon couldn't help but smile.

"It's okay," Gallileon said, "but we're hardly

helping Pepina by standing around here talking."

"Quite true," agreed Cesar. "But what are we going to do?"

"We'll go and rescue her, of course," Gallileon replied.

Cesar looked up at him questioningly. "But how?" he asked.

"I don't know," admitted Gallileon, shaking his head. "I guess we'll have to find out when we get there."

"Get where?" asked Cesar, who was beginning to tremble. "You mean, go to th-th-the pond?" he stammered.

"Where else?" said Gallileon.

Cesar frowned. "I'm not a very strong animal," he said glumly. "I don't have claws or sharp teeth or a pointy beak. And I'm small for my age. I wouldn't stand a chance against a bunch of geese."

"I'm not suggesting that we just crash in and start fighting," said Gallileon. "We can just go and watch, like I did a little while ago. Maybe we'll have a chance to grab her when no one's looking."

"But what if they see us?" Cesar protested. "Then they might hold us captive, too."

"Do you have a better plan?" asked Gallileon.

"Why don't we just tell someone?" Cesar suggested.

"We could round everybody up and go there as a big group."

"We could," said Gallileon, "but they would hear us coming from far away. Plus, I don't want my mother to find out about it. It would worry her too much. We got ourselves into this mess, so we should be able to get ourselves out."

"Speaking of which," said Cesar, "I can't get out of my pen, so I guess I'll have to help you from behind the scenes." Secretly, Cesar was relieved to have an excuse not to go. Of course, he really wanted to help Pepina, and he longed to be a hero, but he was a gentle soul who never so much as hurt a bug. He didn't see how he could be of any use in a fight with Prattle.

But instead of saying goodbye, Gallileon flapped up onto the iron latch that kept the pen shut and pushed off with his feet. The door swung wide open. "Well, that problem at least is solved," he said. "C'mon, Cesar, let's go!"

Cesar spluttered, unable to hide his surprise. "Oh, well! My goodness! Well, in that case, I suppose . . . but then again, I don't know . . . ," he said doubtfully. "I'd probably give you away. I'm not the most graceful of animals."

Gallileon shrugged, pretending it made no

difference to him. "All right, then," he said, jumping down and turning to go. "If you don't want to come, I'll go on my own. But if you never hear from me or Pepina again, you'll know what happened."

Cesar watched with a lump in his throat as Gallileon began to walk away. He thought about what the ducks had said about him and how Pepina had stood up to them. He thought about how Gallileon and Pepina were the only animals who had ever visited him. He thought about his own fear and how much more frightened Pepina must feel, being even smaller than himself. As he thought about these things, something began to grow inside him, something he had never felt before. It was like

he had swallowed a whole hive of bees and they were all buzzing around angrily inside of his belly. Then they buzzed around inside of his head until he could no longer hear his thoughts.

Finally, when Gallileon was almost out of sight, Cesar did something completely unexpected. With his pen a mess, his coat all dusty, and his heart fluttering, Cesar bolted out the door and ran harder than he ever had, toward a place he would never before have dared to go.

Chapter 21

The Standoff

Prattle had Pepina cornered. There had been a long chase, during which Babble and Gabble had watched silently. Now Prattle had finally backed Pepina onto a stone that reached over the edge of the pond. He tossed the old napkin at her. "Now," he snarled, out of breath, "either you put this on, or you walk the plank."

Pepina looked behind her, eyeing the green, scummy water. She looked at the dirty, wrinkled, yellowed rag that lay before her. It had gotten even more soiled during her tussle with Prattle. She couldn't bear the thought of putting that thing back over her head.

Prattle took a step closer. "Some gratitude you've shown us! We offer you the best that we have and you throw it on the ground like a spoiled brat.

Didn't your mother teach you any manners?" he hissed.

At the mention of her mother, a great sadness welled up in Pepina. How she longed to be home, surrounded by her little sisters again. All she wanted was to crawl into Leila's soft nest and snuggle up to her (even though she was really too big for that). When it occurred to her that she might not ever make it back home or see her beloved family again, Pepina began to sob.

"Don't try any of your filthy tricks," sneered Prattle. "After all, it's just a new set of clothes. Hardly anything to cry about."

A voice cut in from behind them. "Then why don't you leave her alone, if it's such a small thing?"

All the geese turned in surprise. Pepina looked through her tears. She was puzzled to see Nip standing just a few feet away. "That's hardly any way to treat your new member, is it, Prattle?" he asked.

"Who asked you, pip-squeak?" said Prattle, bristling with anger. "You're just a lowly guard. And why have you left your post?"

"I'm not a guard anymore. I quit!"

"You what?!" yelled Prattle. He stared at Nip, frozen with shock and fury.

Nip pulled Pepina away from the pond. He placed her down next to a large golden corncob. "Here you are, Pepina," he said. "I don't suppose they've been feeding you around here, have they?" Pepina looked up at him in confusion. Wasn't this the same duck who had dragged her here?

Babble made sounds of regret. "I forgot the poor dear might be hungry," she said sorrowfully.

"That was very considerate of you," said Gabble.

"It was ridiculous of you!" shouted Prattle, running over and kicking the cob into the pond. "What in the world has come over you?"

Nip ignored him. He turned to Babble and Gabble. "My, you ladies look lovely today," he said.

"Why, thank you!" they chimed. They almost never received compliments.

Prattle, taken off guard by Nip's odd behavior, was torn between anger and confusion. "That's enough!" he cried, stamping his big, webbed foot. "You're fired, Nip! Banished! I don't want to see your scrawny beak around here *ever again!*"

"Oh my!" mocked Nip. "A temper tantrum. I'm soooooooo scared. Whatever shall I do?" The geese, who had never seen anyone talk back to Prattle, looked at him with wide eyes.

"Fine!" snapped Prattle. "I'll give you something to be afraid of. Babble! Gabble! Seize him!"

Babble and Gabble looked at Prattle, then at Nip. They shifted uneasily from one foot to the other. Pepina looked around. *Maybe I can make a break for it!* she thought. She got ready to run.

"Well?" roared Prattle. "What are you waiting for?"

Nip stared at him. "They're waiting for you to treat them with a little respect," he replied. "Just like all of us. You're no leader, Prattle—just a bossy, mean coward. Imagine, a big goose like you picking on an innocent little chick like Pepina. It's time for a new boss around here. And I'm the duck for the job."

Prattle was so angry he began to swell up like a balloon. "How dare you!" he wheezed. "You're an ungrateful, impish, pea-brained little twit. Who is going to follow orders from Nip the Nitwit?"

Nip looked him squarely in the eye and said, "The question is, why did we ever listen to you? I can't believe I took any part in this. But I intend to make up for my mistake." Nip walked over and picked up Pepina's bow in his beak. Babble and Gabble watched sadly as he slipped it gently over her head. They didn't want to see Pepina go, but they couldn't force her to stay. "Come on, Pepina," Nip said. "Get on my back. I'll take you home."

Then Prattle pounced.

Chapter 22

The Fray

As soon as Prattle jumped on Nip, Pepina began to run as fast as she could away from the pond.

"Now's our chance!" whispered Gallileon, who had snuck behind the rocks where the geese lived and had been watching the argument. "You take care of Prattle, and I'll grab Pepina."

"Okay!" said Cesar, who had hidden beside him. "You can count on me!"

Gallileon raced across the pond bank until he was just a few feet behind his sister. "Pepina! Over here!" he cried.

Prattle spun around, holding Nip by the back of the neck. Cesar charged into them headfirst and knocked them into the pond.

"Hurry!" cried Gallileon. "Climb on my back! We don't have much time!"

Pepina hopped up as quick as lightning. "Oh, Gallileon!" she said. "Am I glad to see you!"

"Me too," panted Gallileon, looking around for a way out. The pond was in front of them, steep hills were on either side, and a collection of large, sharp rocks were behind them. They were as good as trapped.

Prattle came out of the pond and shook his feathers off angrily. Nip, looking like a soggy dish towel, crawled out behind him. Cesar ran toward Gallileon and Pepina. "Come on!" he yelled. "Let's get out of here!"

"How?" cried Pepina.

Prattle marched slowly and menacingly toward them. "Come on, geese!" he shouted. "Grab her!"

Babble and Gabble didn't move a muscle. They seemed to be frozen, their eyes wide and their mouths gaping.

"Leave us alone!" yelled Gallileon. "The game is over!"

"I'll say when the game is over," sneered Prattle. "In fact, it's just beginning. Why don't we play a little game of hide-and-seek? Pepina can be on my team. We're going to fly to a place far, far away . . . and see if you can find us!"

"You wouldn't dare!" Cesar snorted.

"Oh, wouldn't I?" Prattle laughed. He stopped three feet in front of them. "Tell me one good reason why I should stay on this dinky little farm."

Babble and Gabble snapped out of their daze. "What are you talking about?" asked Babble.

"You're going to leave us?" asked Gabble.

"But why?" the geese said in unison.

Prattle turned to face them. "You really are dim, aren't you?" he said. "After the news gets out about this, no one on the farm is going to like us geese anymore. And why would I stay with you turncoats, you traitors? Whose side are you on? Theirs, I see. So the answer is YES, I'm leaving. Now that I've decided, I have no interest in staying at this dinky pond, listening to the two of you yammer on day after day about the same old things. You sound like a couple of broken records! All you care about is gossip and goslings. But since you don't have any goslings, I never get any rest! So one day I try to give you what you want, a playmate, and you turn on me! And you expect me to stay with you? Not a chance!"

Babble and Gabble stepped back with a gasp. They never knew Prattle disliked them so much. Babble began to cry, making deep-throated honking sounds, while Gabble glared at Prattle.

Nip limped up from the pond and stood by the geese. His feathers were rumpled, and his beak was covered with mud. "You've had your fun," Nip said. "Now, let them go."

"Woo-hoo! This is rich!" cried Prattle. "My ex-officer telling *me* what to do. Along with a couple of good-for-nothing geese, a scrawny rooster, and a tough little piggy. Hahahaha! What's next? Have you got a scary ladybug with you?"

"We may be smaller than you," said Gallileon, "but there's no way we're going to let you take Pepina."

"My, my!" mocked Prattle. "Look who's all grown-up now! Gallileon the clown! I'm surprised to even see you again, after what you did to the sun today. Where did you go after you left the well, eh? Back to Mommy?"

"He didn't do anything wrong!" yelled Pepina. "It was *your* dirty trick!"

"Oh, ho ho! The pip-squeak speaks!" laughed Prattle. "You mean to say you think we geese have power over the sun? I guess you're not quite as smart as I thought after all. Tell me, dear, how could we have made the sun disappear?"

Gallileon had an idea. He spoke slowly and softly. "No, Pepina, he's right. *I* was the one who stole the sun."

Cesar gasped. "That can't be true!"

Pepina looked at him in shock. "No way!" she said.

"It's true," Gallileon said. He looked Prattle square in the eye. Prattle looked surprised.

"So, you're finally owning up to it, huh?" Prattle said. "See, Pepina? Your brother isn't as perfect as you think!"

"No, I'm not," said Gallileon. "In fact, I am very dangerous. What I did today at the well was just, as you said, a demonstration of my powers. But if you don't leave us alone, I am going to sing a song that will make the sun disappear forever!"

The geese honked with worry. "Oh no! Don't do it!" they cried.

"If you let us go in peace, the sun can stay," said Gallileon.

"Nonsense!" cried Prattle. "You don't have any such powers! The sun would always rise and set without you roosters. You just like to take credit for it."

"Then why did you make Gallileon sing at the well if it doesn't mean anything?" asked Cesar.

"It was a trick!" yelled Prattle. "A brilliant plan! I just wanted to show you once and for all how foolish the whole thing is! Roosters are useless, and that's that!"

"A trick, huh?" said Gallileon. "Then how do you explain what happened to the sun?"

"You'll have to ask the cat," Prattle chuckled. "He's in on this, too. But I'm tired of wasting my breath with you fools. Hand over the chick!" Prattle took a step toward them.

"That's it!" shouted Gallileon. "Now you'll be sorry!" He stepped backward, until he was leaning against a large rock for support. Pepina slipped off his back and looked at him. "Don't worry," he whispered. "I won't let anything happen to you."

Gallileon took a deep breath, shook out his feathers, raised his head to the sky, and began to crow at the top of his lungs. He cried with all his might, again and again. His crows rang through the air, just as they had earlier by the well. The geese, the duck, Pepina, and Cesar all looked at him in wonder. Then they looked toward the sky. Even Prattle was a bit worried. After a moment, a shadow fell across them. Gallileon paused. Prattle gasped. The geese began to shake with fear.

"What on earth is going on here?" boomed a voice as loud as thunder. Lester was standing on a large rock above them, blocking the light. Prattle's eyes widened in terror when he saw the dog. He froze.

The Fray

Like a furry orange thunderbolt, Lester leapt down from the rock. "I'm sure this has something to do with you, doesn't it, goose? You're always causing trouble around here!"

"Help me!" screamed Pepina. "Prattle kidnapped me! He wants to take me away from the farm!"

"Whaaat?!" barked Lester. "We'll see about that! Come over here, goose!"

Babble and Gabble panicked. Shrieking and honking, they flapped their wings and began to run about, kicking up a cloud of dust. Lester tore around like a whirlwind, barking, "Just wait until I get my paws on you, Prattle! I'll make goose pie out of you and have you for dinner! Show your face, you sneaky rat! You can't hide from me!"

As the dust settled, Pepina could gradually make out the shapes moving and groaning before her. Cesar was sitting on Babble, who was making strange gurgling sounds. Gallileon was clinging to Gabble, who was trying to shake him off. Lester was pacing and sniffing around furiously. "Where's that goose?" he roared.

Nip limped over. His face was badly bruised, and one of his wings hung to the side. "He's gone," said Nip.

"What?" cried Lester. "He got away?"

Nip nodded. "I saw him fly away right after you jumped down. It's no surprise. I always knew he was a coward."

"Well, what in the world was he doing with a little chick?" Lester barked.

"He wanted to turn me into a goose!" said Pepina.

"A what?" growled Lester.

"You must be joking!" said Gallileon.

The geese, who were now gray from the dust, hung their heads. They began to weep and honk in regret. "We're so sorry!" Babble cried. "We didn't mean for this to happen!"

"We just wanted a daughter, and someone to play with," sobbed Gabble.

"And Prattle said Pepina would want to stay with us because she couldn't go back home," sniffed Babble.

"What?" cried Gallileon. "Why not?"

"Because of the trick," said Gabble. "The egg lips!"

"Egg what?" asked Gallileon.

Eli slipped out from behind a rock. He had quietly observed everything. *"Eclipse,"* he corrected. "It's a rare event, when the moon gets in the way of the sun. It casts a shadow that makes it look like the sun has gone for a little while. I told the geese about it this morning, thinking that they could send out a warning so nobody would be frightened. Instead, Prattle used that information to set up Gallileon to make a fool of himself in front of the entire farm."

"I *knew* they were up to something!" said Pepina. "That's why I followed them. I was going to warn you, but I got caught."

Gallileon jumped up and down. "So it really *didn't* have anything to do with me! And the sun *wasn't* angry!" he cried. "Well, why didn't you just tell me, Eli?"

Eli looked at him with understanding. "That's what I hoped you'd learn when I sent you to observe the geese. I also wanted you to see Pepina, although I knew we'd need more strength to actually rescue her. Which is why, after speaking with Nip, I told Lester there was something fishy happening at the pond."

"So *he's* the one animal Prattle is afraid of!" exclaimed Nip. "Thanks to you, Eli, I now have a broken wing to mend."

"That's what comes from kidnapping helpless little chicks," Eli replied coolly. "Besides, you wanted to be boss of the pond, and now Prattle's gone. It's the perfect opportunity."

"Thanks, but no thanks," said Nip. "It's not worth it."

"Maybe you should elect me," joked Pepina.

"Oh yeah?" laughed Gallileon. "And just what would you do if you were in charge of the pond?"

"Well," said Pepina, "the first order I would give is for someone to take me home. After being kidnapped, half-drowned, dressed in rags, and finally rescued, I am starving!"

"Oh, the poor dear," cried Cesar. "Well, I'd better go, too, then. It *is* getting late! And I'm also a bit nibbly, I must admit. What with all the excitement, I completely missed supper." He turned to go.

"Wait!" cried Pepina, hopping quickly over to Cesar. "I haven't had a chance to thank you yet!" Smiling, she slipped her treasured red-and-white polka-dot bow from around her neck and handed it to the pig.

Cesar's eyes lit up. "F-f-for me?" he stammered. He looked at Pepina in surprise, then shook his head politely. "I couldn't!"

Pepina placed the bow in the pig's gaping mouth and gently pushed his jaw shut. "I want you to have it," she said firmly. "After all, you helped rescue me."

Gallileon and Lester looked at each other and smiled. "It looks great on you!" said Gallileon, chuckling.

Cesar blushed and bowed his head. "Sanku," he said. "Sanku vury mush!"

"Well," said Lester, in an unusually cheerful voice, "it's been nice chatting, but I have to get back to my rounds!"

"See you tomorrow, Cesar!" said Pepina, giving him a quick peck on the cheek.

Gallileon patted the pig on the shoulder. "And thanks for all your help!" he crowed.

Cesar grinned proudly, the bow dangling from his teeth. "Ood-eye, evury un!" he said, then turned and trotted off happily.

Lester bent down, scooped Pepina gently into his mouth (after the fish smell, dog breath was a welcome change), and set off. Gallileon walked beside them, thinking with every step how grateful he was to have his sister back. Several times he tried to tell her just how glad he was, but the words got caught in his throat. He coughed.

"Are you okay, Gallileon?" asked Pepina.

"Fine, fine," Gallileon muttered, blushing. "How about you?"

"I'm all right," Pepina said, smiling broadly, "thanks to you!"

Gallileon coughed some more. "I think I breathed in some dust," he said weakly. "I'm really fine."

When they got close to the chicken coop, Lester put Pepina down so she could walk the rest of the way. "Thank you, Lester," she said. "I owe you one."

"It's all in a day's work." He grinned. Just then, Mrs. Rosa rang the dinner bell, and Lester bounded off.

Chapter 23

Back Home

When Gallileon and Pepina squeezed through the hole in the fence to the chicken yard, Leila rushed up and began clucking. "What took you so long? You're filthy! Aren't you hungry? Your dinner's ready!"

Before either of them could answer her questions, she pushed them toward a pile of bugs. "Don't say a word," she said. "Just eat! Your baby sisters are already in bed. It's late. You must be so hungry!"

They did as they were told. Dinner was delicious. Gallileon was sorry he ate so fast—he hardly had time to enjoy it. Pepina thought she had found heaven in a June bug.

Leila watched them with satisfaction. "So, did you enjoy your first day out of the yard?" she asked Pepina. "I must admit, I got rather worried when I couldn't find you earlier. It seemed the whole farm was at the well, watching that strange spectacle in the sky. Where were you when that happened?"

Gallileon and Pepina looked at each other. "Ummm . . . ," they said.

Just then, a magnificent rooster strutted into the yard, wearing a beautiful blue sash and ribbon.

"Hello, everyone!"

Magellan walked proudly toward his family and gave Leila a peck on the cheek. "How are you all doing? I heard from Lester you did a great job waking the sun today, Gallileon!"

"Thanks, Papa," said Gallileon.

"My oh my!" said Leila. "That's really something, to get a compliment from Lester!"

"And how was your day, my little one?" Magellan said to Pepina. "What did you do? Play in the yard with your sisters?"

"Actually, this was her first day out of the yard," said Leila, smiling proudly. "Her brother took her out."

"Goodness! Well, how did you like that, Pepina? I'll bet you had fun together," said Magellan.

Gallileon and Pepina looked at each other and giggled. "Yeah," said Pepina. "It was almost more fun than I could handle."

Gallileon crowed with laughter. "Haha, yeah! Same here!"

Leila looked both pleased and confused. "It's been kind of a strange day. The oddest thing happened to the sun, Magellan."

"It was the egg lips!" cried Gallileon. "Did you see it, too, Papa?"

"*Eclipse,*" Pepina corrected. "It's when the moon blocks our view of the sun."

"Oh, is that what it was?" asked Leila. "I thought it was a cloud that was going to storm but didn't. I worried that I had made a mistake in sending you out there when I saw that, but I'm glad the two of you have learned to get along."

"Really? No fighting? Wow!" said Magellan. "Pepina and Gallileon playing together *and* an eclipse of the sun. It seems like everyone has had as exciting a day as I have!"

"Yes," yawned Pepina. "And I'm beat. Could I please be excused?"

Magellan looked at her with surprise. Pepina usually talked nonstop at dinner.

"Of course you may," said Leila.

"And me too?" asked Gallileon. "I'm sorry. I'm not used to waking up so early."

"Welllllll, sure, but doesn't anyone want to hear how *my* day went?" said Magellan, slightly disappointed.

"I do," said Leila. "You can tell me after you eat some supper." She smiled, pushing a pile of his favorite food, grasshoppers, toward him. "Good night, Gallileon. Good night, Pepina!"

"Good night!" cried rooster and chick, walking gratefully to bed. As they settled in on the comfy straw, they looked at each other. To Pepina, Gallileon seemed different from when they had set out over the fence that morning. He was still skinny, and his feathers stuck out more than ever after the day's adventures, but he seemed somehow more handsome. He looked almost, well, strong and courageous, two words she would never before have used to describe her brother. *I'm probably just tired,* she thought. *I'm imagining things.* As Gallileon gazed at his sister, he silently thanked his lucky stars that she was back home safe. He noticed, as she scooted deeper into the straw, that she looked different. She was still short and fluffy, but somehow she seemed more . . . grown-up. He closed one eye and then the other and cocked his head, trying to spot what had changed, but he couldn't place it. He sighed and settled into bed. *I'll check again tomorrow,* he thought. *It's probably just a trick of the moonlight.*

As brother and sister drifted off into a delicious sleep, they could barely hear the excited, honking voices of Babble and Gabble in the distance. "Three cheers for Majestic Magellan!" cried the geese. "He has won first prize at the fair! Hooray for Gallant Gallileon, who woke the sun while Magellan was gone! And praise Plucky Pepina—a braver and more fashionable chick could not be found! We must sadly inform you all that Prattle has left Rosa Farm, but we will continue to deliver breaking news around the clock. Thank you and good night!"

*   *   *

Prattle never showed his face again on Rosa Farm. But years later, when Gallileon had chicks of his own, a traveling dormouse told them he had seen the goose on an abandoned farm, with a pond all to himself. Rumor had it, the frogs weren't too happy. . . .

•THE END•